TROUBLE IN PEACEFUL VALLEY

Center Point
Large Print

Also by Barry Cord and available from
Center Point Large Print:

Sheriff of Big Hat
Two Guns to Avalon
A Ranger Called Solitary
The Long Wire
Dry Range
The Iron Trail Killers

**This Large Print Book carries the
Seal of Approval of N.A.V.H.**

TROUBLE IN PEACEFUL VALLEY

Barry Cord

CENTER POINT LARGE PRINT
THORNDIKE, MAINE

Originally published in the US by Ace.
Originally published in the UK by Hale.

The text of this Large Print edition is unabridged.
In other aspects, this book may vary
from the original edition.
Printed in the United States of America
on permanent paper.
Set in 16-point Times New Roman type.

ISBN: 978-1-64358-984-8 (hardcover)
ISBN: 978-1-64358-988-6 (paperback)

The Library of Congress has cataloged this record
under Library of Congress Control Number: 2021935086

TROUBLE IN PEACEFUL VALLEY

-I-

He was a man past the age of impulsiveness, and the flat crack of the rifle, sounding from somewhere behind the low hills to his left, brought him up slowly from the crouched position where he had been examining the cracked shoe on his horse's left forefoot. Now he stood narrow-eyed, a tall, rather slender man with a steel-wire give to his frame.

The first shot was still trembling in the chill morning air when the others came—two whipcrack sounds made by the same rifle. To his trained ear they evoked the picture of a man who had missed his first shot and was laying two fast ones after a moving target. That much he surmised.

Matt Vickers waited. He had the light gray eyes of a thoughtful man, and the blunt jaw of a man with a sure knowledge of himself. A trim brown mustache added a few years to his thirty. He wore a plain gold band on the small finger of his left hand; it was the one touch of sentiment he allowed himself.

A Colt .45 Frontier model was hidden under the skirt of his coat. The plain black leather holster was tied down on his thigh, and it marked him in this violent land where the law was usually on the side of the man strong enough to enforce it, and where a gun was the final arbiter.

The shots had come from upstream, and they were not repeated. He thought, *Trouble? Or just someone taking pot shots at a persistent coyote?*

Vickers knuckled his jaw. He was not here by chance, and he had a sudden hunch that the shots, coming from the direction in which he was headed, had not been fired at any coyote.

He pondered once more the letter he had received in El Paso.

Dear Matt:

I was going to wire Jake Bowles to look into the trouble in Peaceful Valley. But Jake stopped a bullet in Laredo, and it will be a while before he will ride again.

I received a note from Sheriff Earl Wright up in the town of Gunsmoke. He wants a Deputy U.S. marshal, and he sounds frightened. He didn't say what the trouble was. Just wants someone from our office up there. He made his request urgent, but he doesn't want it known that he's called in outside help. Keep that in mind when you ride into Gunsmoke.

The enclosed note is from a man who

signs himself Jed Sayer. He sounds like a crackpot. Do what you like about this.

The letter had come out of the regional United States marshal's office, and a note was enclosed—a penciled scrawl on a ragged piece of brown wrapping paper. It read:

Dear Sir:
    All hell's fixin to break loose up here. Sheriff's scairt to make a move. I ain't. I fit Injuns an' polecats before, an' no bunch of masked tinhorn killers is gonna run me off my place. Send a man down to my place an' I'll tell what I know. Don't let the sheriff in on it. He ain't worth a tinker's dam. Don't send no dam fool either. I don't want to have to bury him. My place is on Copperhead Creek. If he's a good man he won't need more directions.

Yores truly,
Jed Sayer.

Vickers glanced at the brooding hills. A gray overcast sky made a dismal arch over them. The November wind had a sharp edge to it, coming off the first snow on the higher peaks.

The rifle shots seemed to hang like vague question marks in the raw, still morning.

Matt had come to Peaceful Valley from the south, and it had been easier to turn aside to look in on Jed Sayer first than to reach Gunsmoke. He did not share headquarters' feeling that the note was from a crackpot—it had the sharp, true ring of an old codger wiser in the ways of this violent land than most newcomers.

He pulled his Winchester out of its saddle scabbard, levered a shell into place and slid it back. Then he mounted and turned the chestnut upstream. He rode slowly, a man not given to panic or reckless curiosity. . . . The ring on his finger was a constant reminder of one day of heedless anger.

Fifteen minutes later, he rounded a limestone outcropping and came into sight of a small shack set back about a hundred feet from the creek. He pulled up, rested his hands lightly on his pommel and surveyed the two saddled horses which stood slack-hipped before the weathered structure. A light spring wagon with newly painted red wheels was drawn up by a sagging tool shed.

He saw no one, and he guessed the riders were in the shack. He kneed his chestnut forward, and the animal's shod hoofs rang on sunken stones as he splashed across the creek.

The sound brought a man to the door of the shack. He was a short, wind-scoured man with a stubble of gray beard on his cheeks and tobacco stains around his thin-lipped mouth.

He went stiff at the sight of Vickers riding up. His stubby figure blocked the doorway. He glanced past Matt, searching the bare dun hills behind him, his eyes uneasy.

Vickers eased out of the saddle and faced him. His coat was open, and the butt of his Colt showed itself to the suspicious man in the doorway. But a gun was worn by most men in that country, and there was little in Vickers to alarm the man.

Matt's voice was pleasant. "You Jed Sayer?"

The stubby man let his hand come up and rest lightly on the butt of his Colt. "Maybe." He nodded. "Who are you?"

Matt sensed the caution in the man. His eyes kept moving past Matt to the creek and beyond. About them, over the shack, the silence was complete.

"You sent for me," Vickers said. "If you're Jed Sayer you'll remember."

The man stood stubbornly in the doorway. He was nervous. "I don't remember sending for nobody," he growled. "If you're looking for Jed, why don't you say so?"

Someone—or something—whimpered in the gloom behind him.

The deputy marshal frowned. "Someone hurt in there?"

The short man gulped. His eyes made a swift,

expectant search behind Vickers. He said, "Naw. Just a pup."

The whimpering was more distinct, overriding the stubby man's growl. Vickers took a step forward. "Let's take a look," he suggested coldly.

Shorty's gun hand jerked. The muzzle of this Colt was still in his holster when Matt's front sight hooked under the third button of his dirty shirt, snapping his mouth. Fear licked up swiftly in his faded blue eyes.

"Let's step inside," the deputy marshal said mildly.

The man let his Colt slide back into his holster. He pulled his hand away as though the butt were red-hot and stumbled backward, muttering a thin curse.

Vickers followed him inside.

-II-

Light streamed in through two oiled paper windows. The shack, just one big room, was crudely furnished with fittings apparently handmade by the owner, except for the small stove. On the bunk built against the side wall sat a boy, his back resting against the rough, unpeeled logs. He was a thin, narrow-shouldered boy with a mop of reddish hair and freckles splashed across a tear-stained face. His feet were tied. He was crying the way a pup whimpers when it is left alone.

"Cut him loose!" Matt ordered grimly.

The short man hesitated. Matt took a step toward him, his gray eyes narrowing in bleak anger. The man nodded. "Sure—sure—"

He knelt beside the boy and cut the rope, then turned to face the Deputy U.S. marshal. "Didn't mean to hurt the boy," he mumbled. "You one of Riley's gunslingers?"

Matt Vickers frowned. Obviously this man was not Jed Sayer. He said grimly: "No, I was just riding by." He saw faint relief in the short man's eyes, and then a gravelly voice behind him snapped:

"Drop that Colt, fella."

Vickers stood very still. The man behind him,

whoever he was, was light on his feet. Matt hadn't heard him come up. But there was no mistaking the warning in that rough tone.

Vickers opened his hand, and his gun made a soft thud on the earthen floor.

The stubby man kicked it across the room and whirled to face the door, his relief mixed with anger.

"Darn you, Brazos!" he berated. "I thought you'd never show up!"

The man he called Brazos chuckled indulgently. "Saw him ride up, all right," he admitted. "But what the heck, Willy—I thought you could handle him."

Vickers started to turn. He heard a quick, light step behind him and over his shoulder caught a glimpse of a chopping motion. He caught the dull glint of a Colt as it made a swift arc toward his head.

He ducked, and the gun cylinder raked across his skull, knocking off his hat, sending a burst of colored lights dancing in front of his eyes. He kept his feet, however, stumbling toward the man who had hit him. He struck out blindly and felt his knuckles ram solidly against Brazos' cheek.

Willy closed in on him then, kneeing him in the stomach. As Vickers doubled up, he heard the stubby man sneer: "This feller thinks he's tough, Brazos."

Brazos' Colt came down across Matt's head

14

again, sending him face down on the earthen floor. He felt the cool earth against his cheek, and a black fog swirled across his eyes. He put out his hands, palms down, to raise himself. A boot crashed against his side. He twisted and with a last surge of blind energy raised himself to one knee.

Brazos kicked him in the face!

The boy made his break then. He ran with a limping gait, sobbing as he ran past the two men. He made the cabin door before either of them was aware of his going.

Willy caught up with him at the edge of the creek. Grabbing the boy by his suspenders, he yanked the youngster backward and cuffed him roughly across the mouth.

Brazos came toward them, leading the two saddled horses. "Let's get out of here," he growled, "before some other fool happens by and horns in on what ain't none of his business."

He grabbed the boy by one shoulder and the slack of his pants and heaved him up into the saddle. Then he mounted behind him.

Willy turned to glance back at the cabin. "What about him?"

The powerful Brazos shrugged carelessly. "He's not going to cause us no trouble. Just some pilgrim who wandered off the main trail." He grinned humorlessly.

"Might be he was lying," Willy muttered. "Could be one of Riley's men."

Brazos guffawed.

"He's dressed like a dude," Willy said, bristling. "But he wears his holster thonged down, and the way he got his gun out—"

Brazos cut him off with a curt, "All the better then." He turned his bay away from the cabin. Willy kneed his cayuse alongside. The sounds of their departure faded slowly in the chill morning. . . .

The chestnut waited patiently by the door. The cold wind came across the bare yard, across the small, empty corral. The grays hitched to the spring wagon moved restlessly, their harness clinking softly.

The chestnut walked to the door and thrust his head inside. He was too big to enter.

He saw Vickers sprawled on the dark floor, and a questioning sound fluttered in his throat. He saw the deputy marshal stir, roll over, push himself up and stagger drunkenly against the wall.

For Matt the shack was spinning in a slow, off-center whirl. The pain over his eyes made him squint.

He took a deep breath, and pain knifed through his bruised side. He felt unsteady enough to rest momentarily against the wall while he touched

16

the side of his jaw where Brazos' boot had landed. Then he explored the cut over his left ear. He felt blood under his fingers, matting his brown hair around the gashed lump.

He smiled. He was a man most dangerous when he smiled. And it had been a long time since he had been so brusquely manhandled. It would not happen again.

He found his hat and set it carefully on his head; then he went down slowly to his hands and knees and found his Colt, kicked under a bunk. He checked it carefully before sliding it into the holster.

The chestnut whinnied softly. He was still blocking the light through the door. Vickers walked to him and ran his hand gently over the sleek muzzle.

"Real tough hombres," he murmured. He leaned against the saddle for a moment, gritting his teeth. Then he looked around.

The grays hitched to the wagon shook themselves with increasing impatience.

Vickers closed his eyes. Pain hammered in his head. He pushed away from the chestnut, walked to the creek and wet his handkerchief. He wiped the blood from his chin and washed the cut over his ear.

He began to feel well enough to think. What had happened didn't make sense. If the short man was Jed Sayer, then his note had been a trap.

But why? Why had he sent for help in the first place?

He remembered the rifle shots, and now he tied them in with Brazos, the burly man he had only glimpsed. Brazos had been outside the cabin when he had ridden up. *Doing what?*

Matt started walking along the creek, looking for signs, and in a sandy stretch he saw where the two men had turned right, heading through a narrow gap between low hills. A hundred yards beyond this he came to a brush-choked ravine.

From where he stood, which was practically in the tracks of the rifleman, he could see a body partially hidden under low mesquite bushes. He could make out a wide groove in the earth, as though the man whose body rested there had dragged himself to his present position before he died.

It gave Vickers an insight into the mental attitude of the man who had fired the rifle shots. He had little doubt that Brazos had killed the man whose body lay hidden there. Brazos must have stood on the edge of the ravine and watched the man run—and shot him as he would have shot a jackrabbit taking off down the gully.

Vickers went down for the body.

Ten minutes later he pulled the man's own blanket over the stiff features of a gray-headed, partially bald, spare man who even in death had the lean, stringy, red-necked look of a farmer. His pockets were empty, offering Matt no hint of his identity.

He could be the father of the boy who had been crying in the cabin. Or maybe *he* was Jed Sayer. Or both.

After he had placed the dead man inside, Vickers closed the cabin door. He walked over to the waiting team, unhitched the grays and turned them loose. The man inside the shack was dead; there was nothing more Matt could do for him now. Perhaps the sheriff in Gunsmoke would know him. But Matt had decided not to ride into town with the body. A body attracted attention— and until he had a talk with Sheriff Earl Wright, Matt wanted no attention.

He mounted the chestnut and turned his glance downstream to the fall of the wide valley stretching to the horizon.

"Peaceful Valley," he murmured. He touched the lump on his jaw. "Reckon it needs a bit of currying."

-III-

Deputy Dan O'Malley shoved open the law office door and tramped inside, shouldering aside a slight, spectacled man in his hurry. He didn't apologize for his rudeness, and Bertrand Musick, county attorney, let his spiteful gaze linger on the deputy's blocky shoulders before he closed the door and went out.

Two loafers playing checkers close to the pot-bellied stove looked up as Dan paused beside them. The deputy's square-jawed face was as tight as a hide stretched over a tom-tom. He jerked a thumb doorward.

"Out!"

The slack-jawed players craned dirty necks to look at the sheriff, whose boots were propped up on the corner of his desk. Earl Wright, a fleshy middle-aged man, had a genial smile and a back-slapper personality. He was a politician first, a lawman second.

He dropped his booted feet to the floor, and a frown pulled his light brows together over a whiskey-veined nose.

"Now, Dan," he started to remonstrate, "no need to—"

"What I have to say I want to say in private!"

20

the deputy snapped. He turned his grim glance to the checker players, who rose hastily, spilling counters on the floor. He waited until they had gone, then walked to the desk and placed his hands on it, leaning forward to look into the older man's scowling features.

"I just heard you let Big Sam Fisher out of jail!"

The sheriff made a pacifying gesture. "Had to, Dan. We couldn't hold him. Even Musick said—"

"Him!" Dave's voice surged with contempt. "We haven't had a conviction since Spur put that shyster in office!"

"Now, now," the sheriff soothed him, "Musick can't convict a man without evidence. He'd be laughed out of court if he tried."

"Sam Fisher killed Noel Travis!" Dan snarled. "Isn't that evidence? He was positively identified as one of the bunch of killers who rode up to Travis' place, called him outside and shot him!"

"Who identified him?" the sheriff cut in. His voice was uneasy, and he avoided the deputy's angry gaze.

Dan O'Malley straightened slowly, white showing around his tightened lips. "You know darn well who saw him! Travis' boy, Buzz, saw him—that's who!"

Sheriff Wright leaned back, his eyes clouding. "Sit down, Dan," he invited him heavily. "This is going to hit you hard."

Dan remained standing, his face becoming whiter.

"Buzz has disappeared," the sheriff said. "He left home with his uncle, Ben Cavanaugh, about four yesterday afternoon. Ben said he wanted the boy to stay with him now that Buzz was alone. This morning Ben's wife came in. Ben and the boy didn't get home last night."

A visible shock went through Dan O'Malley. "Not the kid, Earl. Not Buzz."

The sheriff wet his lips. "When are you going to quit butting your head against a stone wall, Dan?" His tone was placating, but it held an uneasy note. "Forget the Travis killing. I don't think anything serious happened to the boy. And if we lay off, if we forget about Sam Fisher, Buzz will turn up."

"So Spur runs you, too, Earl?" Dan's voice was shaken. "I guess I always knew that, didn't I?"

"You talk like a darn fool!" the sheriff snapped back. He was aroused now, and all the more angry because he realized that much of what his deputy said was true. "I don't know what happened to Ben and the boy. But even if Buzz was back in town, it would still be a nine-year-old boy's word against that of Rita Coleman and Big Sam. Remember, Dan, the Coleman girl herself swore that she and Sam were in town the night Noel Travis was killed, picking up supplies at Caleb's store. Musick and I checked with

22

Caleb. He backed the Coleman girl's story."

"Ivor Caleb will say what Spur tells him to," Dan snarled. "And Rita Coleman, not her father, runs Spur!"

"Maybe," the sheriff admitted. He thrust his heavy-featured face across the desk. "You used to work for Spur once. What made you quit? Rita? Or Ann?"

The deputy's eyes seemed to become blue chips of glass. "What happened at Spur is my business, Earl. Don't ring Ann Coleman into it!"

"I'm not ringing anyone into it," the sheriff protested; "just advising you to forget it. The Colemans won't—"

"The Colemans aren't bothering me now," Dan cut in bitterly. "It's a kid—a crippled boy who saw his father shot down like a dog; a boy who had the nerve to name the killer, even though he was a Spur rider. What's bothering me, Earl, is the absurd mockery Spur has made of the law in Peaceful Valley!"

Wright turned away, a displeased look on his face, but his deputy's flat-toned anger followed him.

"We're the law in Peaceful Valley, Earl. We've got badges to prove it!" Deep scorn rang in his voice. "But we can't keep men like Noel Travis from getting killed. We can't even keep a killer like Big Sam Fisher in jail!"

The sheriff whirled around, his face contorted with anger. The deputy's words had stung. "Dan, why blame me? What can *I* do? What can *you* do?"

"I jailed Fisher," Dan reminded him. "I took Buzz into town and found him a place to stay at Amy Lawson's boarding house. He was going to testify against Big Sam at the trial." The deputy sneered. "Then you sent me down to Spokesville on an errand you could have done by mail. Why, Earl? To get me out of the way?"

"Yes, you darn fool!" the sheriff exploded. "I was thinking of your hide. You got Big Sam by pulling a gun on him when he wasn't expecting trouble. How long do you think you'd last the next time you tried it?"

"Just long enough," Dan flung back grimly, "to settle for Noel, and maybe for Buzz Travis now." He shook his head, anger smoldering in his eyes. "How long do you think you can straddle the fence, Earl? What happens when Jon Riley and Milt Gavel move across the Longhorn, move against Spur? Five thousand head of sheep, Earl, backed by a dozen paid gunmen! Gavel's out to win this time! What do you do then?"

The sheriff sank wearily into his chair. "If those sheep move across the Longhorn, I won't be responsible," he said. "It's Spur range they'll be moving onto, Dan. Coleman will have a right to fight back with hired gunmen of his own!"

"And you and I will just sit back, Earl? We'll let all hell break loose?"

"What more can we do?" The older sheriff's tone was bitter, resigned.

Dan reached up, unpinned the badge from his coat and dropped it on the sheriff's desk. "I don't know what *you* can do," he admitted coldly. "But I'm through making a lie out of this tin star. If I can't make it mean anything, then I don't want to wear it."

"Don't be a hot-headed fool!" the sheriff growled. "As long as you wear that you've got some protection. Without it—"

Dan's smile was bleak. "Without it I'm fair game, eh?" He took a hitch at his gun belt. "I don't like Spur, Earl. I don't think I ever did, even when I worked for it. Spur has run this valley so long the Colemans think they own it, and the people in it, too. For the first time since the Comanches quit raiding out of the Tuscaloons, Spur's in trouble." His laughter had an ugly edge. "Big trouble, Earl."

Sheriff Wright's voice was harsh. "Think what you like about Spur, Dan. But if Jon Riley and Milt Gavel move across the Longhorn, the law will be on Spur's side."

Dan sneered. "What law, Earl?"

The sheriff held back his anger. "You've quit," he pointed out stiffly. "You have no right to question me."

Dan nodded. "All right, Earl—you back Spur. All I want to know is why Noel was killed. Why was Jed Sayer killed? Why those two small-time farmers? I know *who* killed Noel. But I want to know why. I think it's because of what happened to Jon Riley."

Sheriff Wright's face went gray. "You fool!" he whispered. "You stick your nose into that, and you'll be dead!"

He watched Dan wheel away and slam the door behind him. He settled back in his chair, feeling trapped, feeling very old. . . .

Dan O'Malley, balanced on the edge of the plank walk, let his bitter gaze range along Gunsmoke's Main Street. His anger was still alive, a frustrated sour anger that made his mouth mean. Thinking of young Buzz Travis and what might have happened to the boy, he felt sick inside.

A rider had appeared at the far end of the street where the statue of Sam Houston on horseback pointed across a small square of green to the courthouse. The rider jogged toward him.

Sooty clouds had thickened during the day, and now the deputy caught the smell of rain in the raw wind that nosed along the street. He thought sourly, *It's gonna be a bad night,* and felt restless and combative.

The rider came on toward the sheriff's office, and Dan let his belligerent stare slide down the stranger's bruised face. He was dressed cleanly and was smooth-shaven, except for the small brown mustache under his nose. A gun showed under the skirt of his coat. The man looked sure of himself, despite the recent beating he seemed to have taken.

A stranger in Gunsmoke! And at this point of time in Gunsmoke's violent history, all strangers were suspect!

He put his gaze on the deceptively broad shoulders, let it rest briefly on the late model Winchester in its scabbard under the rider's left leg.

A confident man, Dan decided resentfully, and the big chestnut under the stranger earned a second look. *That horse is probably worth a quarter of my year's pay,* Dan thought bitterly, and let that bitterness lie in the regard he rested on Matt Vickers.

Matt swung the chestnut toward the walk and dismounted by the sheriff's rack. He dropped reins over the weathered pole, and the animal nosed him affectionately as he passed by.

Matt's eyes rested on Dan's angry face for a brief and impassive moment.

"The sheriff in?"

Dan nodded grudgingly and stepped off the walk, moving around to his rangy grulla, which seemed run-of-the-mill next to the big chestnut. He mounted and cast a last look at the stranger disappearing into the law office.

Wonder who you are? he thought angrily. *One of Spur's new guns, probably.*

He felt a helpless irritation take hold of him. There were too many strangers in the valley these days, too many hard-faced men wearing tied-down holsters. The tension this created was like a fog settling over Gunsmoke; like the gray and uneasy dawn before a big battle.

He shook off the thought, narrowing his thinking down to his own problem. He had two choices before him now—drift or stay. He thought of Buzz Travis, and the choice was hard.

Somehow he felt sure the killing of Noel Travis was the beginning of still greater trouble to come, that it was connected with Jonathan Riley's return to Peaceful Valley. He knew that much, although he knew nothing of what had happened the night Riley had disappeared from the valley more than eighteen months before.

The sheriff knows what happened that night, Dan thought grimly. *Earl knows more than he lets on. And he knows what brought Riley back.*

He was cutting around Sam Houston Square when he heard riders. He lifted his glance and held it on them as they came into town at a run, heading for him. Leading them was a lithe, leather-jacketed figure mounted on a beautiful white horse.

Rita Coleman rode into Gunsmoke in that

manner, as if she owned the town. She was a medium-tall, nicely rounded girl who rode like a man and who, some said, ran Spur now that her father, Colt Coleman, was laid up.

A riding quirt hung by her right leg. With it she was almost as dangerous as a man with a gun at close quarters. She saw Dan O'Malley and cut her horse in ahead of his grulla, forcing him to rein in sharply. He caught her disdainful smile as she flashed past.

A length behind her rode Ira Cobb and Owen Sales. Spur men, known everywhere as bodyguards for the Coleman girl.

Dan checked his cayuse, swiveled in the saddle, and watched the Spur outfit race down the wide street. He felt the burn of an old humiliation, and a sudden impulse made him turn around and slowly follow.

-IV-

The sheriff was looking through old tax notices, but he was not reading them. His thoughts were on his wife and children, and he was trying to put down the uneasiness his deputy had aroused in him.

He heard his office door open, but he didn't raise his eyes from the papers. Only when the footsteps paused in front of his desk did he straighten and look up—into a pair of the coolest gray eyes he had ever seen.

The stranger's gaze dropped from his face to the badge still lying on the desk where O'Malley had tossed it. Quickly, the sheriff's blunt fingers reached out and scooped up the metal star, which he dropped into a desk drawer.

He looked at Matt, his voice truculent. "What do you want?"

"You sent for me," the man before him said. "I'm from the United States marshal's office. The name's Matt Vickers."

Sheriff Wright's eyes widened. He ran his gaze over the man, noting the bruised face, and a streak of skepticism curled his lips. He put his doubt into words.

"I asked for help. But I expected more than one man." Bitterness flared briefly across his soft face. "I don't see where you—" he glanced toward the closed door and lowered his voice— "what you can do here, Vickers."

"Let's give it a try," Matt suggested. His voice was easy, yet it held an odd timbre that made Wright sit up and eye him closely again.

"What's your trouble, Sheriff?"

Sheriff Wright eased back, scowling at the gray light seeping through the windows. Any day now, the first snow would come sweeping across the valley from the high range, and Earl Wright hated winter with a soft man's love of comfort.

"Sheep!" He muttered the hated word distastefully. "Five thousand of them, waiting to cross the Longhorn!"

He saw a frown gather in the deputy marshal's eyes and got up, pushing an almost empty box of cigars toward his visitor. "Sit down, Marshal, while I fill you in on the trouble."

He walked to the door and locked it, while Matt took a cigar and settled back.

The sheriff turned slowly; then his hand came up, and there was a Colt in it. The look he put on Matt had a tremulous uncertainty.

Matt waited, cigar poised in front of his mouth. The silence dragged on between them until Matt said thinly, "You don't trust me, Sheriff. It's got you so scared you don't trust anyone."

"I sent for help," Earl whispered. "I'll believe you when I see something more than words."

31

Matt shrugged. He clamped his teeth on the cigar, reached carefully inside his coat pocket and brought out his wallet. He flipped it open, and Wright came forward, his gun cocked. He looked at the identification, his mouth working, his lips framing the words he read.

"Here's more," Matt said evenly. He replaced the wallet and brought out the United States marshal's letter. "You ought to recognize this, Sheriff."

Earl nodded. His shoulders sagged, and he let the hammer of his Colt down easy. He holstered the gun and walked back to his chair.

"Acted like a jittery old fool," he apologized. "I'm sorry."

"I'm a careful man myself," Matt said. He reached inside his pocket and brought out a match; he lighted his cigar. "You were saying?"

"Yeah." Earl's voice held a tired ring. "Long as I can remember," he began slowly, "cows and Colt Coleman's big Spur spread have been in Peaceful Valley. Coleman branded his first calves when the Comanches were raiding out of the Tuscaloons. He fought off the red devils, and he fought off rustlers. In twenty years there's not much he doesn't own or control in the county."

He watched Matt's face, but there was little he could read in the deputy marshal's features.

"The Longhorn comes out of the brakes in the high country by the foothills and leaves the

32

valley through Comanche Pass. The Longhorn is as far as Spur range goes on the north. There's little except scrubby rock valleys beyond it."

The sheriff squirmed slightly in his chair, as though the retelling made him restless.

"Milt Gavel has run sheep back of those hills almost as long as Spur has run cows in the valley. Five years ago Milt Gavel and his brother Chris tried to shove sheep across the Longhorn. Spur met them head on. Chris was killed." Wright made a small gesture. "Milt's been waiting for a chance to get even ever since."

Matt said nothing. The sheriff was faced with an old problem, he was thinking: a man too soft for the job expected of him.

"So far it's an old story, Vickers," the sheriff muttered. "But now Milt's got himself a new partner, a man named Jon Riley. And he's come back with a dozen gunslingers to force a river crossing!"

"Who's Riley?"

Wright made a limp gesture. "Funny thing about him, Matt. Riley used to be a schoolteacher here in the valley." He caught Matt's look, the slightly raised eyebrows, and he added harshly: "As nice a gent as you'd ever expect to meet. Colt Coleman himself was responsible for bringing Riley here. Hired him after reading an ad he saw in a Boston paper. Riley seemed to get along right well with the Colemans, too," the sheriff said. "I even heard talk that he was courting Coleman's younger daughter, Ann."

"What happened to Riley?"

The sheriff shrugged. "I don't know." He avoided Matt's gaze. "Just disappeared from town one night about eight months ago. Didn't even pick up his personal belongings. They're still in his old room at Amy Lawson's boarding house."

Vickers got to his feet. "You mean a man who used to teach school here disappears, then shows up a year and a half later as a gunman? Comes back as a sheepman, ready to start a range war with Spur; with his old friends, the Colemans?" The marshal's tone was puzzled. "Why, Sheriff? Why would Jon Riley hate Spur that much?"

Earl Wright fumbled with papers on his desk. "I don't know," he insisted. He kept his eyes away from Vickers. "I don't know what caused Riley to change. But I do know he's not the same man I used to know. He's turned killer. Wears a gun slung low—and he's learned how to use it!" His tone rose with uneasy impatience. "All I can tell you is that he's back with Milt Gavel and a dozen killers. And if he isn't stopped, the hot place's gonna be a pleasanter spot than Peaceful Valley!"

"You talk with Riley?"

Wright's face seemed to sag. "I tried. I rode up to the camp across the Longhorn. I didn't even get a chance to cross the river."

Vickers reached for his hat. Then he remembered the dead man in Jed Sayer's shack—and the boy who had been crying.

"Do you know a man named Jed Sayer?"

Wright seemed to shrink back in his chair. His eyes went muddy, as though he had been caught concealing something. He licked his flabby lips.

"Yeah, I know Jed."

"A fairly tall man, gray hair, mole on his left cheek? Looks like a farmer?"

Wright shook his head. "That's Ben Cavanaugh. Where did you run into him?"

Vickers told him, told about finding the body he had left in Sayer's cabin. He was remembering Jed's warning, and he did not tell the sheriff why he had gone to Jed's place.

The sheriff's face was gray. His cheeks sagged. "The boy was Buzz Travis." He straightened under Vickers' probing look, and his lips tightened harshly. "They've gone too far," he muttered. He seemed to be summoning his courage, fighting a deep-rooted fear.

A knock sounded on the door. Then someone began to pound on it. A voice yelled: "You in there, Earl?"

Wright lumbered to his feet. "Marshal," he said tensely, "come back tonight. Around nine. The office will be dark, but the door will be unlocked. I'll be here, waiting. I'll tell you everything then, about Jon Riley and all of it, Marshal."

35

He was at the door now, snicking the bolt back. One of the checker players Dan O'Malley had chased out shuffled in and stared uneasily at Matt Vickers.

"Heck, Earl," he mumbled, "we didn't know yuh had company. We just thought—cripes, it's cold out there."

Vickers said evenly, "Thanks for setting me straight about that trail south, Sheriff." He pushed past the two men in the doorway.

The sheriff stared after him, feeling his newborn courage ooze out of him. Capable as he might be, Matt Vickers was only one man. And the guns facing him were many.

Earl Wright felt a little sick as he turned and walked back into his office.

The deputy U.S. marshal rode up Main Street, turning to eye the three riders who swept past him. Rita Coleman gave him a bold, appraising look, her head tilted back and challenging. She seemed to expect every man to look at her. The two men with her gave the marshal a lidded scrutiny as they rode by.

Farther up the main thoroughfare, the blocky youngster he had seen standing in front of the sheriff's office was riding back slowly, pulling his grulla toward a saloon rack.

Vickers rode on, noting this and slipping it to the back of his mind. He left the chestnut at the livery stable and came back to Main Street, carrying his bag.

It was dusk now, with the sky darkening fast in the east. A deeper black was spreading down from the north. Vickers could feel the chill dampness of the wind against his face.

A three-story building across the road advertised itself as the Stockman's Hotel. He set his bag down, then remembered the sheriff's reference to the Lawson boarding house where Riley had once lived.

The problem of Riley had his interest. He was about to turn into the barbershop and inquire where he could find the Lawson boarding house when he saw the three riders coming back along the street. They seemed to be searching for someone.

They pulled up before the rack of the saloon across the street, and the girl remained waiting in the saddle, idly flicking a long-lashed quirt in one hand while the two men dismounted and went inside.

Vickers pulled his attention away from her. He picked up his bag and was headed for the shop when a man and another girl came around the corner, the girl's laughter ringing somewhat shrilly in the dusk.

The man was young, not more than twenty, Vickers judged—slim, good-looking and quite drunk. He had lost his hat, and brown curly hair tumbled carelessly across his forehead. He had a narrow, weak-chinned face.

His arm was around the waist of the girl—a Mexican girl, even younger than himself. She was trying to keep him from weaving all over the walk.

". . . Fooled her," Vickers heard him say, his voice boastful. "Can't get around without a chaperone, eh? Know what, Juanita? I'm not trusted off the ranch alone at—Whoa!" He steadied himself, eyeing Matt, who had stopped in front of him.

"You're blocking my way, fella," he said. He tried to make his voice tough, but it was only a boy talking, a boy made bold by liquor.

Some old hurt was visible in Vickers' gaze. The ring on his finger seemed to pinch him warningly. It was an illusion, he knew, yet it brought up out of the mists of time the vague features of his young wife, hurt, shocked, twisting with the pain of the bullet. . . .

A kid like this one, talking big. A late afternoon in a town a long way from here—a time more than eight years ago. A kid talking big and wearing a low gun, calling Matt a liar, calling him yellow. He was new to his job—a sheriff's deputy—and he had his pride.

He might have avoided the fight; a thousand bitter moments afterwards he wished he had. But instead he had shot it out with the young killer, and the long dark hand of Fate had seen fit to have his wife come running up the street just at that time—stop, press back to watch. And the kid, dying, had fired one aimless shot.

The shot had killed his wife.

The youngster's boastful voice picked up at his apparent hesitation. Vickers roused himself.

"Sure, son," he conceded. "Just stay put, and I'll go around you."

"Say, you're a gentleman." The youngster grinned. "Allow me—" He bent forward in a sweeping bow, lost his balance and stumbled forward.

Vickers caught him before he could rub splinters into his face. He straightened the youngster up, steadied him. His grin matched the one on the boy's face.

"You want to watch the cracks in the boards, son. They can fool you."

The whip that curled over his right shoulder stopped Matt Vickers short, as its flicking tip left its thin bite on the youngster's cheek!

Matt whirled just as the quirt came down again. Holding it was the girl he had seen pull up at the saloon rack across the street.

He jerked aside and forward, his fingers closing on the thick butt end of the quirt as the lash cut through the air. He jerked roughly, pulling the angry girl off balance as he twisted the quirt out of her hand.

Rita Coleman stepped back, calling to the two men coming at a run from across the street. "Ira! Owen!" Her voice was imperious, outraged.

The two Spur riders came at Matt Vickers. Ira, tall, lanky and wire-tough, moved in fast, ahead of Owen. He drove a looping right for Matt's face, missed, and the force of the blow spun him part way around.

Vickers hit him twice—jolting blows that spun Ira Cobb completely around, slamming him against the barbershop window. The Spur gunman went through the sash with a jangling of breaking glass.

Owen, ten feet away, paused, his hand jerking for his gun.

A flash, a roar, and a rolling cloud of smoke sheathed Vickers' right thigh. Owen's Colt hand jerked. His fingers fell away from his gun butt, which he had barely touched. Blood made a dark pattern across his torn knuckles.

It was over before it had gotten fully under way. The youngster Matt had kept from falling on his face was swaying on his feet, his fingers still lifted to the whip cut on his chin. The Mexican girl had backed against the wall, where she cringed in fright.

Ira Cobb hung dazedly across the window still. Behind him, outlined in the lamplight, the barber, a short hairy man, was standing over a customer, razor held high in his hand in a moment of frozen indecision.

The deputy U.S. marshal turned to Rita Coleman, who was standing at the edge of the walk. The quirt lay at her feet. Vickers picked it up and looked at her, and the boss of Spur flinched at the look in his eyes.

"You're quite impulsive with this, ma'am," he drawled. "A taste of your own medicine might tame you down a bit!"

"You wouldn't dare!" the girl cried. Her voice was high, and there was uncertainty in it. "I'm Rita Coleman! My father owns Spur!"

"He must have spoiled you something awful," Vickers said. He took a step forward, and the girl took another step backward, bringing her to the edge of the plank walk. Behind her was a hitchrack where a mousy bronc lifted his head in sleepy curiosity.

The youngster's laughter was a jarring note in the stillness. "Why, sis? You're not afraid of him, are you? Not my own dear bossy sister?"

Rita whirled. Panic made her judgment faulty. She misjudged her closeness to the edge of the walk and stepped off before she could stop herself. She twisted to regain her balance and fell face forward across the hitchrail. For a ludicrous moment she hung there, balanced precariously— and Matt Vickers found the temptation too much for him.

He dropped the quirt and stepped forward, his left hand bearing down hard on the girl's back, holding her across the pole. His open right hand came down hard across the straining seat of her Levi's. He administered two more brisk paddlings before he stepped back.

The girl's face was a mottled red as she regained her feet. Tears of anger and embarrassment fell slowly down her cheeks.

"You—" Her words were not those used by a lady. They came shockingly through the gathering dusk, wild and shrill. Then she caught herself, pulled her voice down to a whisper.

"You're dead, mister!" The effort at control made her voice sticky. "If you're still in town tomorrow, you'll be dead! No man can do what you've done to me and live!"

She turned to the youngster who had called her "sister." Her voice was still shaken, but she had regained some of her authority. "Ken! Come here!"

The youngster held back. He looked at the slim-waisted Mexican girl he had been squiring around town. It angered Rita Coleman; it brought out in her an old prejudice, an arrogant superiority. "Don't look at her, Ken! Remember who you are—at least for a moment or two!"

Ken Coleman brushed his hand across his face. He was now sober, and soberness left him no match for his strong-willed sister.

Rita reached into her pocket, dug out two silver dollars and tossed them contemptuously to the Mexican girl. "There's your pay—now git!"

The girl looked down at the money, then at Ken's indecisive features. Then she turned in a whirl of bright-colored skirts, ran back to the corner and disappeared.

Ken Coleman lifted his eyes to Matt, and defiance touched his lips. He made an odd gesture of salutation, touching his fingers briefly to his forehead.

"Turn down an empty glass for me, stranger," he murmured.

"Ken!" His sister's harsh voice cut him off.

He shrugged and went over to her. She turned to Owen, who was standing off the walk, holding a handkerchief to his bullet-scarred hand. "Ken will ride your mare, Owen," she said. "Get that hand attended to, and take care of Ira. You can pick up Ken's horse at the livery later and ride back to the ranch."

She took her brother's arm possessively and marched him across the street to the horses at the saloon rail. She helped him mount, then swung into the saddle of the trim white gelding. She rode with her weight in the stirrups, keeping high off her saddle.

Vickers watched them vanish into the darkness at the far end of Main Street. Ira Cobb had pulled himself away from the shattered window and was

43

leaning weakly against the wall beside it. But Owen was watching Vickers, making no move.

Matt turned to pick up his bag. Behind him a voice hailed him sonorously.

"Stranger, let me buy you a drink! I've been waiting to see that Coleman girl taken down a peg for nigh onto nine years!"

-V-

Moving out of the crowd was an imposing figure in a black frock coat and white shirt with a black string tie. An incongruous silk hat was perched precariously on a thatch of bristling white hair. He was steadying himself with a silver-headed cane, and at ten paces Matt Vickers could smell the sour whiskey on his breath.

The deputy marshal said: "Later, mister." He indicated his bag. "I'm on my way to the Lawson boarding house."

"Tut-tut!" The paunchy figure held up his palm in a pompous restraining gesture. "Let H. Goldwyn Pepper, Gunsmoke's most able attorney, take care of it for you."

He turned and called to a wide-eyed boy who had witnessed the brief action in front of the barbershop: "Tommy, take the gentleman's bag to your ma's rooming house and tell her she has a new boarder. I'll bring him along in time for supper."

Vickers hesitated. The dark-haired boy came up and bent over his bag. "Gee!" Tommy exclaimed. "You going to live with *us,* mister?"

"Call me Matt," the deputy marshal said. He gave the boy two bits and added gently: "Tell your ma I'll be much obliged for the room, Tommy."

H. Goldwyn Pepper cleared a path through the group on the walk with his stick. "Out of the way, boys! Judgment Day has come to Peaceful Valley. The powerful Spur is at last receiving retribution."

Matt Vickers frowned. This man's pompous way of expressing himself seemed as out of place in the valley town as did his incongruous get-up.

All of them turned into a saloon several doors away—a dingy hole with a short varnished bar, a few chairs and tables and an atmosphere sour with spilled beer. Two range-clad men with feet on the rail glanced at Pepper and the deputy marshal, their faces hard in the lamplight. They edged slightly away as Pepper breasted the counter.

"A drink of Taylor's bonded!" Pepper ordered loudly. He banged his fist down on the bar, then turned to Vickers. "Kentucky's best, feller. You from the South?"

"Way south," Vickers replied, wondering how he could shake the man without offending him.

"Come from Georgia myself," Pepper said. He raised a hand and wagged it. "Always claimed if we had a few more men like them Texas Volunteers with us that day at Chickamauga—"

The bartender slammed the bottle down in front of Pepper and slid two glasses beside it. "You've been fighting that battle since I've known you," he growled. "When you going to quit, Pepper?"

46

Matt grinned. The lawyer ignored the bartender's gibe. He slid a glass to Vickers, slopped whiskey into it. "Drink up, boy. Nothing but the best for—for—"

"Name's Matt Vickers," the deputy marshal supplied quietly.

"Vickers? Just leave the bottle, Ike," Pepper admonished the bald-headed bartender. "Vickers? Hm! Heard that name somewhere before."

"You live at Lawson's?" Matt asked.

"Amy's place? Sure. Nicest place in town. Nothing like that flea-bag hotel across the street."

"Know a man named Riley?"

He was watching Pepper but saw instead the flicker of interest in the eyes of the two range-clad men at the end of the bar.

"Riley? Ex-schoolteacher? Sure. I know Riley." Pepper finished his drink and poured again. "Lived right across the hall from me. Only educated man in town. Shakespearean scholar—" He hiccupped, eying his companion closely. "Heard Riley's back. All set to cross the Rubicon, he is."

"Cross which?" Vickers muttered.

"The Longhorn." Pepper waved a hand deprecatingly. "Just like Caesar, son—he's waiting to cross the river. When he decides to cross—"

"What happened to Riley?"

Pepper wiped his lips with his coat sleeve. The

deputy marshal caught a glimpse of the man's eyes then—blue and hard and incongruously alert in that slack, time-eroded face.

"Spur ran Riley out of the valley a year and a half ago," the lawyer said. "Biggest mistake Spur ever made!"

"Why?" Vickers probed. He was interested; the problem in Peaceful Valley had undertones. "Why did Spur run him out?"

Pepper turned away, reaching for the whiskey bottle. His groping hand knocked it over, and he stared at the whiskey making its run down the counter.

"Don't rightly know," he said stiffly. He set the bottle upright and reached for the marshal's glass. "Have another, Matt?"

Vickers shook his head. He had turned to go when he remembered the man he had turned aside at the northwest end of the valley to find. The sheriff had made no mention of Jed Sayer, but Matt was curious.

"Know where I can locate a man named Jed Sayer?" He asked the question casually, as though it were an unimportant afterthought.

Pepper dropped his foot from the brass rail. "Jed?" His voice was oddly sober in that moment.

The U.S. marshal nodded.

Pepper made a slow gesture toward the rear of the saloon. "West of town, Matt. In Boot Hill."

His surprise didn't show in Matt's eyes—or in his voice. "When did it happen?"

"About three months ago."

"You sure?"

"Saw him myself." The attorney frowned. "Noel Travis brought him into town. Travis and Jed were neighbors up on Copperhead Creek. Travis said he found Sayer in his corral—seems like Jed was kicked to death by his ornery mule." Pepper put his attention on the glass he was refilling, but his voice held a sharp edge of surprise. "Did you know Jed Sayer?"

Vickers shook his head. "Must have been another fellow I had in mind."

He turned away, feeling the uncomfortable silence that gripped the grubby bar as he closed the door behind him.

On the corner Matt paused, feeling the first splatter of rain slant against his face. So Jed Sayer was dead? And so, he remembered, was the man who had found him—Noel Travis.

Something here didn't match up with what he knew. Something was wrong with the pattern. For Jed's note, forwarded to him with the letter from headquarters, had been dated less than a month ago!

Either Jed was not dead, or someone else had written that note, using Jed's name. But Vickers could see no reason anyone would want to do that.

Nor had he gotten any closer to knowing what had brought Jonathan Riley, one-time valley schoolteacher, back to Peaceful Valley as a gunman.

He checked a nagging impatience, remembering that he had an appointment with Sheriff Wright. Whatever was frightening Gunsmoke's sheriff, he'd know about it tonight. . . .

He turned the corner, and a shadow moved up to him as if it had been waiting for him to show up. A hard voice asked:

"Got a light, mister?"

Matt looked the man over. The blocky frame was familiar, but the shadows hid his features. A little farther on a saddled horse nosed the walk, waiting.

Vickers reached in his pocket for a wood match, moved in closer to the building to avoid the rain, and thumb-nailed it into flame. In the reddish glare he saw the man's face—square-jawed, sandy-stubbled, a thin white scar on the side of the jaw.

The man bent to the flame, the limp cigaret between his lips. He took a drag, and the cigaret glowed. He said, "You work for Jon Riley?"

Vickers let the flame go out and dropped the burnt match to the walk. The rain was coming down harder now, and a thin spray touched his cheek. Somewhere down the dark narrow side street, a loose shutter banged.

"No," he answered shortly. The man whom he now recognized as the sheriff's deputy, Dan O'Malley, persisted coldly, "I saw how you handled Rita Coleman and her watchdogs. You're not a Spur man." There was a question in the statement.

"No."

"Strangers handy with a gun like you are," O'Malley muttered, "don't come to Peaceful Valley for their health. You got business here?"

"Maybe," Vickers murmured. "What's it to you?"

Anger roughened Dan's tone. "Might be a lot!" he snapped. "I'm the law in Gunsmoke!"

Vickers smiled bleakly. "I don't see a badge on your coat, bud."

"I turned it in!" Dan growled. "Me and the sheriff don't see things the same way."

"Maybe you need spectacles," Matt suggested dryly. He took a step away, and Dan put a hard hand on his arm. "Now wait a minute, feller—"

Vickers turned. His tone was suddenly flat. "You want answers, son, you get that badge back!"

He walked away, leaving Dan standing there stiff and grim, feeling a deep frustration.

The Lawson boarding house loomed up halfway down the narrow street, a big block of a building with a long flight of outside steps leading to a landing at the second-floor level. The landing was enclosed, to protect the entrance from the weather.

The wooden sign nailed above the street entrance read: *Lawson Boarding House.* A kerosene light hanging below it illuminated the wet letters.

Vickers opened the door and walked into a carpeted hallway, flanked by a curving staircase on his left, a dining room past the archway to his right. Fringed curtains hung in the archway. A clatter of dishes and the sound of voices came to him.

He paused in the dining room entrance and looked over the long table. The meal seemed well attended. A short, stout woman with gray hair was just setting down a platter of boiled potatoes. She looked up as behind her, from the kitchen, a boy's voice rang out excitedly:

"That's him, Ma! That's our new boarder!"

Amy Lawson came over to the U.S. marshal, smiling, wiping her hands absently on her apron. "Mister—?"

"Vickers, Mrs. Lawson," he replied. "I'm sorry I'm late."

"Not too late." She was still smiling. "I should think you'd like to wash."

He nodded, and she turned and called Tommy. "Show Mister Vickers to his room. I'll have him bring you some hot water. And I'll keep supper warm for you in the kitchen," she promised tiredly, "just this once. I don't like to make exceptions. Supper is at six o'clock sharp."

"I won't be late next time," Vickers assured her.

He followed the eager boy up the stairs. His room was at the far end of the hall, close to the door opening to the outside landing. Not too big, he noticed, as Tommy lighted the oil lamp on the small table by the window. But comfortable. And it looked clean.

It contained two Currier and Ives prints of New England winter scenes, a worn but neat counterpane, an oval hand-braided rug on the floor by the brass-knobbed bed.

Tommy paused in the doorway. His eyes were big and shiny as they surveyed the new boarder.

"Gee!" he whispered. Then he was gone as Matt Vickers smiled.

The deputy marshal dropped his hat on the bed and took off his coat. His ribs still pained him where Brazos had kicked him. He grimaced.

The dresser mirror showed him his features, his right cheek bright in the lamplight, his left shadowed. The lump on his jaw was taking on a lemonish tinge. He touched the cut on his head and felt the crusted blood. The ache had receded to a dull background annoyance.

He had been hurt worse, he thought philosophically, and reached for his sack of Bull Durham.

But the image he had studied in the mirror remained with him. He was thinner, and of late he had grown more withdrawn—he knew this about himself. He had felt some of the joy of living seeping from him; the long trails and the rootless nights were beginning to pall.

What made a lawman, anyway?

After his wife's death, he had hated his badge and what he had been called upon to do. He had taken it off and thrown it away, and after the funeral he had ridden out of town. He had gone back just once—three years later. The pain was no longer sharp, but in the brief moment he had kneeled by Lucy's grave he knew he could never stay in that town where he had started a life—and where she had died.

But a man had to live—it was an iron-clad law, forced upon an individual with a healthy body. And he had found that he was not by temperament a sky pilot or a town man. He tried a half-dozen ways of life and eventually returned to the law. The land west of the Mississippi was still mostly frontier, and against the lawless tide moving into it stood men with badges—some of them bad, some weak, but most of them honest.

It didn't pay much. But Matt had never wanted money. It was dangerous, but this did not deter him. Looking back, he wondered why he had taken this job with the United States marshal's office, and found no ready answer. He did not feel that the law as he encountered it was always right, nor did he admire every man wearing a badge, and he had met men the law wanted whom he had admired.

He was back to wearing a badge because he had started out that way; beyond this he could not explain it even to himself. But he wore his wife's wedding ring on his little finger to remind him that anger was a treacherous thing, and that often restraint was the wisest path to law enforcement.

He was almost through his smoke when the boy reappeared, weighted down with a steaming copper kettle. Vickers took it from him and poured hot water into the washbowl. An earthenware pitcher containing cold water stood on the dresser. He added some from this until he had tempered the water in the bowl to his liking.

Tommy was watching him. The deputy marshal felt the eager regard of the boy, who probably had had little opportunity to know his father. Mrs. Lawson, he assumed, was a widow. Widows usually ran boarding houses.

Matt Vickers had his hands up, ready to unbutton his shirt, when he caught a faint blur of movement against the rain-streaked windowpane. He saw it and moved with one instinctive reflex.

Almost simultaneously, as a bullet shattered the pane, the earthenware pitcher on the dresser disintegrated. Halfway across the room, Vickers'

Colt slammed two shots which further reduced the glass in the broken pane. Then he was at the light, blowing out the flame. He whirled to the bedroom again as darkness blotted out everything in the room.

In the stunned silence he heard a faint sniffling, and the equally faint but definite sound of someone running down the outside stairs. Matt got up close to the wall by the window and peered out. Rain gusted into the room, spraying a cold mist into his face. Down in the darkness of the alley below, he thought he saw movement; then it was gone.

As he pulled down the faded green shade, he cursed his carelessness in forgetting even for a moment to be on constant guard.

He scraped a match and relighted the lamp. He could hear frightened, questioning voices from downstairs, moving toward the upper floor. But he was suddenly concerned with Tommy Lawson.

The boy was sitting down just inside the door, propped against the inner wall, and he was holding his left arm. Blood was bright and warm between his fingers. His eyes grew wider when he saw the blood, and his sniffling grew louder.

Kneeling beside him, Vickers pulled the boy's hand away. Relief brushed across his face. There was a tear in the boy's shirt sleeve just above his elbow—a cut about an inch long. But the gash was a shallow one. It had not been made by a bullet; more probably it was the result of a piece of flying crockery.

Amy Lawson appeared in the doorway. Her face whitened as she saw Tommy on the floor, and she swayed a little, steadying herself against the door jamb.

Vickers said quickly: "He's not hurt badly, Mrs. Lawson. Just a cut."

She knelt beside her son, tearing the sleeve away to see for herself. The deputy marshal straightened, closing the door on the curious roomers who had followed Mrs. Lawson upstairs.

She looked up at him, frightened, but reassured that Tommy was not badly hurt. "What happened? How did Tommy get cut?"

He told her.

"But why?" Mrs. Lawson was bewildered. "You've just come to town. Why should anyone care you are here, or want to kill you?"

He was thinking that anyone could have followed him to the boarding house, waited on the outside stairs, and when a light appeared in a darkened window close at hand, easily surmised who was occupying the room.

"I'm afraid I'm a poor risk," he said gravely. He hesitated, wanting to let this woman know who he was, yet deciding against it. It would serve little purpose, and perhaps cause her still greater worry.

"Perhaps I should look for another place," he suggested.

Mrs. Lawson answered distracted, "This is your room, Mr. Vickers. If you wish to stay, I have no objections."

Matt smiled. "Thank you." He knelt beside Tommy and knuckled the boy's jaw playfully. "You're all right, Tommy," he said firmly. "We'll get the doc to put a bandage on that arm. Doesn't hurt much, does it?"

"No, sir," Tommy said, holding back tears. Mrs. Lawson turned to the window, where a gust of wind soaked the shade. "I'll be up later to clean up," she said. "I'm afraid we'll have to board up the window for tonight, Mr. Vickers."

He nodded. "Why don't you take Tommy downstairs?" he suggested. "I'll be long shortly."

He waited until they had gone, then turned and eyed the drawn shade. It had been close, he reflected grimly. He wondered if the ambusher had been the blocky former deputy who had stopped him on the street.

The rain, drumming loudly against the fluttering shade, spread a wet blotch in the room.

Matt shrugged. He took off his shirt and prepared to wash and shave.

The doctor was already in the kitchen when Vickers went downstairs. He had Tommy's arm bandaged. He looked curiously at Matt as the deputy marshal entered the room.

"Nothing to worry about, Amy," the doctor said. "Keep a fresh bandage on it for a few days." He was a short fat man with a brisk manner.

"By the way," he observed, "you may have a visitor. I just saw Jonathan Riley ride into town with Milt Gavel."

He said it quietly as he snapped his bag shut. Tommy looked at his mother, his eyes shining. "Gee, Mom, is Mr. Riley coming back to live with us? Will he take me fishing again?"

Amy Lawson shrugged. She stood, tired and plain-looking, by the kitchen stove, her hands folded in her apron.

The doctor said, "I hope this rain keeps Spur riders out of town tonight." He said it casually enough, but there was an undercurrent of concern in his voice that was probably reflected by most of Gunsmoke's citizens.

He said good night, then walked out. Vickers had turned to follow when Mrs. Lawson called, "I have your supper in the oven, Mr. Vickers."

Matt looked back. "I'm afraid it will have to wait." He caught up with the doctor on the low stoop. The rain beat hard against them, and the medico turned impatiently at the lawman's question.

"Yes. They turned in at Charlie's Saloon. It's up by the Square."

Vickers pulled his hat brim down and turned up

his coat collar. He had not eaten since morning, and he was hungry. But he was more curious to see what Jon Riley, ex-schoolteacher turned gunman, looked like.

-VI-

Dan O'Malley eyed the big chestnut in the stall next to his grulla. The stableman watched him curiously, lantern in hand.

"Nice animal," he ventured. He was talking about the chestnut.

O'Malley shrugged. He had watched the owner of that horse handle Spur in a way no one else in Peaceful Valley had dared. He thought of this and it bothered him, for the slender man with the deceivingly mild appearance fitted into no category Dan knew.

Gun-handy strangers drifting into town were headed either for Spur or Milt Gavel's camp across the Longhorn.

The ex-deputy rubbed the hard angle of his jaw. He had been at loose ends when he had left the law office. His gesture, he now realized, had been one of impatient defiance. When he reflected, he knew there was little he could do about Buzz Travis on his own hook, nor could he bring Noel Travis' killer to justice. And he had the growing feeling that real trouble was fixing to break loose in the valley.

The stableman frowned. "Devil of a night," he muttered, listening to the sound of the rain on the barn roof. He added pessimistically: "Won't

be long, either, before this turns to snow."

O'Malley didn't even hear him. He was deciding that he ought to see Earl, find out who the stranger was and what he had wanted to see the sheriff about.

He nodded then, the echo of the hostler's comment prompting him to mutter grimly, "Yeah, devil of a night."

He ducked out into the rain and made a quick turn to reach the shelter of the wooden-awninged walk. It was midweek, and the rain must have discouraged the few hands who might have made the trip to town. The streets were empty. Light splashes made wan patterns in the puddles.

Dan turned left on Cottonwood Street, and was in the darkness of it when he heard the shots. One—then two quick blasts! He paused, trying to place the gunfire. The rain came down steadily, hammering against the dark buildings; the spouts dripped or gushed into rain barrels.

The night seemed to smother the gunfire, swallow the reports as though they had not happened.

Continuing down the street, the deputy turned in at the sheriff's house. The small picket gate was open. He walked past a flower bed showing only brown stalks and dead pods and knocked on the door.

Louella Wright, a tall, spare woman with a stern, lined face, came to the door. "Earl?" she repeated. "He went out a few minutes ago. I think he went back to the office."

Dan frowned, touching fingers to his dripping hat brim.

"Dan!" she cried anxiously. "Is anything wrong? Earl seemed—he seemed so nervous—"

O'Malley shook his head. "I don't think so, Mrs. Wright." He turned and went down the steps, the dim glow on the wet footpath fading abruptly as the woman closed the door.

He stood by the gate in the darkness, unmindful of the rain. Down the narrow residential street a door opened, throwing a wedge of light over a small stoop. A tall figure came out and paused. The Reverend Sharon, thin and white-haired, showed up behind the tall man.

Surprise kept Dan O'Malley paralyzed by the sheriff's gate. *Jon Riley!*

The wind blew down the street, carrying a brief snatch of words to Dan. ". . . See her first thing in the morning, Jon." It was the minister's voice; Riley's reply was lost in the shifting wind. The door closed, and darkness blotted out Riley's tall figure. In the wet blackness Dan sensed that Riley turned away, heading for the intersection at Main Street.

The ex-deputy hesitated. What was Riley doing in town? What had he wanted with the Reverend Sharon?

Blast it, he thought savagely, *Earl knows*

what this is all about! He's got to tell me!

He pulled his hat down over his eyes. Rain trickled down his neck, and he swore at the discomfort. He came out to Main Street and glanced down its dark, dismal length. Ahead of him, Jon Riley moved down the walk.

A gun blasted, its sound muted as it reached O'Malley; it sounded as though it had been fired inside a building. His hand reached up to his coat where his badge had been. He thought grimly that what was going on in Gunsmoke now was none of his business. Not until he had seen Sheriff Wright, anyway.

He turned left, away from the sound of the shot, and headed at a quick walk for the sheriff's office.

Matt Vickers felt the rain against his face as he headed for Houston Square. The windows of Charlie's Saloon laid their barred pattern across the walk, their light reflecting from the deepening puddles. Four horses stamped in the mud by the rack, their hoofs sucking in the mire.

Vickers found the saloon door, pushed it open and closed it against the rain which, on this side of the street, reached under the wooden awning. He put his back to the door, his glance moving slowly over the big room with its scattering of customers to three men who were bunched close together at the bar.

Charlie's was a more pretentious place than the saloon to which Vickers had been taken by the pompous lawyer, Pepper. It was bigger, and there were several more gaming tables as well as a well-stocked bar. Four girls in short sequined gowns stood in a lonesome group at the far end of the bar.

The three men along the rail looked at the tall deputy marshal as he entered. Matt saw their glance move appraisingly down his rain-soaked length, and felt a sudden alertness take hold of them.

The man in the middle was a short, thick-set fellow in his forties. His dark, surly features were hidden by a gray-flecked beard.

His companions were clean-shaven. Matt instantly judged them to be hired gunslingers. Lean, hard men, their most prominent items of dress, despite the weather, were low-slung guns.

Vickers walked to the bar, crooked his finger to the fat, mustached bartender and asked for whiskey. The three men watched him; there was no belligerence in their stares, only a covert watchfulness.

Matt poured his drink and let it stand. He turned to face them. "Which one of you is Jon Riley?" he asked.

The man nearest him, a round-shouldered, gaunt-framed individual, moved slightly away from the rail, his pale blue eyes swerving to meet Matt's. His right hand hung loosely by his gun butt.

The thick-bodied, bearded man in the sheepskin coat frowned. "Who wants to know? Spur?"

"Not Spur," Vickers said. His voice was flat. He was slightly puzzled, too. Somehow, none of these men added up to the picture of Jon Riley he had framed in his mind.

"I might be Riley," the stocky man said. He had enough whiskey in him to make him slightly reckless. Besides, he was facing only one man, and was flanked by two pretty tough companions of his own.

" 'Might be' isn't enough," Vickers said.

"Why? You got something you want to tell Riley?"

A dangerous smile edged Vickers' lips. He saw trouble gathering in the attitude of these men, in the edgy, chip-on-the-shoulder feeling each wore like a garment. The way they hung together indicated a clannish grouping, and he had the thought that if Jon Riley was not one of these men, they were at least from his camp.

"Yes," he said quietly. "I've got something I want to tell Riley. I want to tell him and his bunch of sheepherders to stay out of Gunsmoke."

The thick-bodied man stiffened. "Well, well!" His voice was an open sneer. "Hear that, boys? This jasper's standing right tall for his size!"

Vickers knew what was coming and didn't wait for it. He took a quick step forward, ramming his shoulder into the blue-eyed gunman next to him and spinning him aside. Matt's left hand moved faster than the bearded man could see. His fingers closed around a handful of the man's coat collar. He had the surprised man yanked up close to him just as the gunster farthest away stepped clear of the rail and reached for his Colt.

Matt Vickers' draw shaded him. His gun blasted sharply, spinning the man about. The gunnie dropped his Colt, his arm going limp. His face twisted into a grimace of pain.

The deputy marshal's leveled Colt kept the blue-eyed gunman from making a try for his weapon. The man was crouched over in the attitude in which he had recovered his balance, his right hand rigid on his gun butt.

Vickers held the thick-set man up close to him, his voice as cold as the beating rain. "Tell me once more, feller—are you Riley?"

He heard the outside door bang open, and a voice snapped cold and clear in that silent room:

"I'm Jon Riley!"

Vickers laid his glance on the tall, cool figure of the man who had just entered. The gun in his fist was leveled squarely at Matt.

The thick-set man he was holding took advantage of the situation and pulled away from Vickers. His voice rang harshly in the stillness.

"Darn it, Jon, where've you been? Who's this jasper?"

His voice faded out. Rain swirled in with a rush of wind, flapping Riley's slicker around his long legs. The gun in his hand was still steady, light glinting from the long barrel.

Vickers studied the lean dark face. Something like a small scar marred the bridge of Riley's nose. His eyes were dark, unyielding. His lips were sensitive, and there was a sensitive flare to the man's nostrils. But there was nothing uncertain or soft about the man's attitude.

"You looking for me?" he asked bluntly.

Matt let the silence between them continue. He had not come looking for trouble, and he would get nowhere with this man through force. He read this in Riley's eyes, and it forced a smile to his lips.

He slid his Colt back into holster and lifted both hands in a gesture of peaceful intent. "I want to talk with you, Riley."

Riley's eyes did not change. "Why?"

"I want to know why you came back to Peaceful Valley. I want to know what happened to you a year and a half ago."

He felt Riley's stare on him, puzzled, weighing him. Annoyance crowded him. He had been forced into a position of disadvantage by the

68

thick-set man eying him with angry hostility.

Why should Jon Riley tell me anything? he thought. *Is this the place to talk?*

A bleak sarcasm edged Riley's reply. "Ask Spur, feller. Ask Rita Coleman."

He made a small motion with his Colt. "Let's get going, Milt. Burke, give Selman a hand. It's a long ride back to camp."

Vickers waited, not making a move to interfere. Milt Gavel gave him a dirty look. Burke, the blue-eyed gunman, walked to Selman, who was holding a wadded handkerchief to his bullet-torn arm. He drew a handkerchief from his own pocket and tied it tightly around Selman's arm, over the blood-soaked wad. He bent to pick up Selman's Colt and jammed it into the wounded man's holster.

Riley stepped aside to let his truculent companions by. His eyes were still puzzled as they regarded the deputy marshal.

"You work for Spur?"

Vickers shook his head. "I'm speaking for myself. Stay on your side of the river." His voice was soft, but it held a definite warning. He started to walk toward the schoolteacher, his boots scuffing softly in the still saloon.

Riley's lips twisted. He didn't lower his Colt. Instead, his thumb slipped the hammer back with a soft click. "Who are you?"

"I'll tell you the next time we meet," the deputy

69

marshal said softly. "In the meantime, stay on your side of the river."

Riley shrugged. "I'm giving Spur a quiet weekend. We're moving across the river Monday. If you're working for Coleman, tell him. And—whoever you are—keep out of my way!"

He stepped back through the doorway into the rain-swept darkness. Vickers stood in the light, knowing he was a good target and knowing that any sudden move might be misconstrued.

He had met Jon Riley, and now, more than ever, he was interested in what had driven a mild-mannered schoolteacher to the brink of a range war with the biggest ranch in the valley.

He waited until they were mounted. He could see them through the open door, dark, blurred shapes in the rain. They wheeled away from the rack, and Vickers came out, stepping quickly out of the light.

Somewhere up the street a muffled shot seemed to ride the wind. Riley glanced toward the sound and shrugged. He was the last to back his cayuse from the rack, whirling to join his companions as they rode toward Houston Square and the dark, muddy trail out of town.

-VII-

Sheriff Wright waited impatiently, his determination fading as the minutes dragged by. He paced the familiar office in the darkness, listening to the rain beat against the windows.

Dan's accusing voice kept ringing in his ears. A badge was no good unless the man behind it made it good; the law was only as strong as the men who backed it.

It was his job to stop the holocaust that was about to take place in Peaceful Valley. He had to get rid of a secret he had been carrying too long inside him. It had gnawed at him for more than a year, devitalized him, rendered him ineffectual in facing up to the problem of Jonathan Riley's return.

He wasn't big enough to stop it, he admitted dismally. Nor was Dan, whose foolhardy courage could only get him killed.

He didn't believe any one man could stop it. But Matt Vickers had a right to know.

He heard the step on the walk outside his office and stopped his pacing. He tensed, feeling the edge of his desk press against his thighs. A hand touched the knob, turned it. The sheriff heard it above the dismal patter of the rain outside.

Caution made him drop his hand to his gun.

He waited, his anticipation squeezed within the cold bonds of his fear. The door opened, and for a moment a tall shadow was outlined against the night.

Sheriff Wright's voice came out in a sigh of relief. "Vickers!"

His visitor did not answer. He had moved inside the office quickly, swinging the door shut behind him. He was lost in the darkness by the wall.

Sheriff Wright's voice probed the blackness. "Vickers?" There was a querulous note in it now.

The shadow moved toward him. Coming into a stray gleam of light from the window, it took on bulk again. Something in the man's hand reflected a note of light. It was a small and insignificant reflection, yet it jerked Earl erect, sent naked terror clawing through his insides.

"You?" His voice was a thin explosion. He sucked in his breath. *"What do you want here?"*

The voice that answered him was pitched low, grim. "You called in outside law, didn't you, Earl? You sent for help from the United States marshal's office? You couldn't play it smart, could you? All you had to do was sit on the fence, Earl; sit there and look dumb. And one day you'd look inside your desk drawer and find an envelope with a thousand dollars in it. For you, Earl."

Earl tried to push back against his desk.

"You've got me wrong," he said desperately. "I didn't tell him anything—"

"You sent for him! I told you what would happen if you—"

"No!" Sheriff Wright's voice was a hoarse protestation. "I—" He sensed it coming and tried to slide away. At the last moment of his life he stopped running and reached for his gun.

The shot was curiously muffled. It didn't sound outside the law office. But the slug caused Earl to sit down hard. He was still trying to reach his gun when the killer stepped up close and fired again.

Earl jerked and shuddered once. The killer crouched by his side, dropping the folded blanket which he had used to muffle his shots. He put the back of his hand to Earl's open mouth. To make sure, he felt for the sheriff's pulse.

He was kneeling over the body when he heard footsteps outside the closed door. He came erect, the naked muzzle of his Remington .44 gleaming faintly.

Dan's voice preceded him into the office. "Earl! You in the office, Earl?"

The killer edged away from the sheriff's body. It was a good fifteen feet to the back door; he knew he couldn't make it in time.

The front door banged open. Dan's blocky figure was momentarily limned against the street. The killer whirled and fired quickly, the .44

unmuffled now, its sound racketing through the dark building.

Dan spun around and fell out of sight on the wet plank walk.

The killer crouched by the sheriff, scooped up the powder-scorched blanket and ran for the back door. He jerked it open, hesitating long enough to make certain the rain-swept back yard was empty. Then he closed the door behind him and faded into the night.

Matt Vickers found the ex-deputy lying on the boardwalk. He crouched over the man, Colt in hand, listening for some small giveaway sound from within the office.

He was not the only one who had heard the shot. Several dark figures loomed up in the street and moved cautiously toward him.

Vickers straightened. He stepped across the walk, flattening himself against the wall near the door. He heard nothing and took the chance no one was inside. He went in fast and ducked back against the inner wall; he waited, gun cocked, and knew that whoever had shot O'Malley was no longer in the dark room. There was an untenanted feeling in the sheriff's office.

Orienting himself from some odd nook in his memory, Vickers moved directly to the wall lamp. He scraped a match on the seat of his pants, and as he brought the flame to the wick, he saw the sheriff's body huddled in front of the desk.

Matt adjusted the wick and reset the glass chimney; the reflector cast its light over the office now. He turned to Earl's body, but he knew the sheriff was dead before he knelt beside him.

A small crowd was gathered outside the law office, around O'Malley, when Matt walked out. One of the townsmen hunkered over the sprawled figure said: "Dan's still alive. Bleeding bad from a hole in his chest, though. We oughta get him over to Doc Ramsey's place right away."

Matt pushed through the group and crouched over Dan. He recognized the wounded man as the hombre who had stopped him on his way to the boarding house; the youngster who had claimed to be a deputy, who had coldly informed Matt that he did not see eye to eye with the sheriff.

Had Dan come back here to have it out with the sheriff? His manner had not been respectful of the lawman.

"Who is he?" He asked the question of anyone.

"Dan O'Malley. Sheriff Wright's deputy."

Matt eased Dan's Colt from his holster. Rain left sparkling droplets on the long barrel. He flipped the cylinder out and eyed the five brass cartridges gleaming in the lamplight from the office. He thrust the muzzle under his nose, verifying what he suspected. The gun had not been fired recently.

Someone who had gone poking through the

law office suddenly exclaimed. "Holy Jumping Jehoshaphat!" He came to the door. "The sheriff's been shot, too!"

The crowd pushed inside for a look. Matt turned and went back into the office, shoving men away from the sheriff's body. He bent over Earl again. The sheriff had been shot twice, yet his own Colt was still in his holster, unfired!

The U.S. marshal was puzzled. He had heard only one shot.

He swung around to face the scowling, muttering men. His voice held the sharp ring of authority. "There's nothing we can do for the sheriff, folks, except get him to the undertaker. But the deputy needs medical attention. Couple of you pick him up and take him over to the doc—"

"Whoa! Who in blazes are you to give orders?"

The man who asked the question was a burly teamster, and the suspicion in his voice was picked up by the others.

Vickers considered the legitimate question. There no longer seemed to be any need for secrecy. The sheriff who had written to headquarters for help was dead. And the man who had killed him probably knew that Earl Wright had written for help.

So Matt shrugged, pulled out his wallet and flipped it open, showing them the deputy U.S. marshal's gold badge pinned to it. "The name's Matt Vickers," he said coldly. "Special investigator from the U.S. marshal's office in Tucson. Sheriff Wright sent for me."

There was a muttering in the group. The teamster sounded skeptical. "What in the world would Earl Wright want with a man from the United States marshal's office?"

"Maybe he thought he could pass the buck to someone else," a thin, celluloid-collared man sneered. He worked as a clerk in Allister's freight office. "Earl liked sitting on the fence. But Jon Riley, coming back with Milt Gavel, must have given him a bad headache—"

"Someone gave him more than a headache." Vickers' tone was short and rude. He looked at the clerk with little friendliness. *Maybe Earl had not been the best lawman in the world,* he thought, but he had little liking for any man who would sneer at a dead man, or belittle a man who had died behind a lawman's badge.

The clerk must have seen this in Vickers' face. He stepped back, flushing, turned on his heel and strode away. Vickers turned to the teamster. "Was the sheriff married?"

The burly man nodded.

"Then you'd better get word to her." He looked at the others standing around uncertainly in the rain. "Some of you get Dan over to the doc's before he catches pneumonia. Get Earl out of here, too—before his widow comes over."

He stood by until the group dispersed. He was acutely aware of the badge in his pocket. Until a new sheriff was appointed or elected, he was now the only law in Peaceful Valley.

The rain was beginning to soak through his coat as he looked gloomily down the darkened street. He knew something of the trouble facing him now. But the pattern was still obscure, clouded by Jon Riley's past.

There were two armed camps in the valley: Riley and the sheepmen across the Longhorn; Spur waiting on the other side.

But something puzzled Vickers. The pattern didn't come together as it should have. He was certain that neither Riley nor the men who had been with him tonight had killed the sheriff. And he had not noticed any Spur riders in town after Rita Coleman and her two bodyguards had left.

Somehow the impression remained with the tall, gray-eyed deputy marshal that Earl had not been afraid of Spur or of Jon Riley, but of someone else.

Matt Vickers decided to look in on Dan O'Malley in the morning. The former deputy had been taken to his room after Doctor Ramsey had dug the bullet out of him. One of the local women was acting as his nurse.

The rain had let up during the night, but the morning was raw and getting colder. Matt turned into the sleazy hotel lobby and climbed the creaking steps to the deputy's room.

Dan was lying in an iron-framed bed, propped high on two big pillows. His eyes were closed. The stout, gray-headed woman dozing on the chair by his bedside awakened as Matt came in. She came heavily to her feet, her attention lingering on the badge Matt had pinned to the outside of his coat.

She started to talk as she moved toward the door, glad of a chance to get away. Dan had spent a restless night, she said, but he was much better this morning.

Dan opened his eyes as she went out. His gaze focused on Matt standing by the foot of his bed. He seemed puzzled by the badge on Matt's coat.

Vickers smiled pleasantly. "Doc said you'd live, so I thought I'd drop over. Feel strong enough to talk?"

The woman poked her head back into the room. "I'll have breakfast for you, Danny, when I come back. Doctor Ramsey said you could have coffee and biscuits, if you felt like eating this morning."

Dan nodded weakly. He waited until she closed the door again. His tone was truculent as he looked at Matt.

"That badge real, mister?"

Matt nodded. "I'm Matt Vickers, investigator for the United States marshal's office in Tucson."

Dan closed his eyes. "Reckon I acted like a darn fool," he muttered.

"A man has a right to his way of thinking," Matt said. He waited until Dan's eyes opened; then he told him about Sheriff Wright's letter.

"Earl was afraid of someone, Dan," he added. "I got the impression from his talk with me last night that there was more to the trouble here than sheep and cows. He started to tell me about it when we were interrupted. So he made an appointment to meet me in his office after dark."

"And I thought Earl was sitting on the fence!" Dan muttered. "I thought he was a Spur man, bought hide and hair by Colt Coleman." He winced as he drew in a breath. "Earl must have known what to expect if it came out he had sent for help from your office."

Matt came around to the side of the bed. "What do you know about Jon Riley, Dan?"

"Nothing much." Dan's lips stretched thin. "Liked him, but—" He flushed. "Heck, I might as well admit it. I wasn't much for schoolteachers. And then, Riley was in pretty thick with Spur, and I—"

"You hate Spur?"

"I've got no use for Spur. Or Rita Coleman."

Matt didn't ask him why. Instead he mentioned Jed Sayer. "Did you see the body?"

Dan nodded slightly. "What there was to see, Marshal. Looked like a bloody bundle of rags—"

He winced again, setting his teeth stubbornly against the pain in his chest. "But I know a bullet hole when I see one, Mr. Vickers, even in a body smashed up like Jed's was. Right between the eyes."

"Then Jed wasn't killed by his mule?"

Dan's eyes said no. He licked his lips again. "I liked old Jed," he went on. He was tiring, and it showed in his voice. "I liked Noel Travis, too. I often stopped by both places when I was riding up along the Copperhead. Jed was an ornery cuss. An old Indian scout, tough as dried leather and independent as all get-out. Didn't want much out of life. Said he'd seen all he wanted an' had all he needed. Had his mule, his piece of land and his buffalo gun. That was enough for him."

Matt grinned, recalling Jed's blunt note. "Salty cuss, eh?"

"Noel Travis was different, Marshal. Dirt farmer turned small rancher. Lost his wife a few years back. Had one boy, crippled in an accident—horse jammed him up against the corral bars just as he was beginning to learn to ride. Noel punished himself for that ever after."

Dan paused and closed his eyes. Matt said: "This Travis boy—is he a skinny redheaded kid with a mess of freckles?"

Dan said, "Yeah, that's Buzz," without opening his eyes. His jaw was set against the hurt inside him. After a moment he repeated the affirmation, and then his eyes snapped open, bright blue and cold. "You find the kid, Mr. Vickers?"

Matt told him about the trouble he'd run into at Jed's place.

Dan's eyes burned with a deep frustration. "I sang this song to Earl, but he didn't listen to me, Marshal. I'm gonna keep singing it. Spur's behind all this trouble. Sam Fisher, Spur's big tough ramrod, killed Noel Travis. Maybe he's the man who killed Jed, too. But we can prove he killed Noel, because Buzz saw him. I had him in jail. But Rita Coleman got him out. Alibied for him. Told the county attorney, a shyster name of Musick, that Sam had been with her at Caleb's Store the night Noel was shot. Even swore out an affidavit. Buzz was the only witness to his father's killing. It was his word against that of Big Sam, Rita Coleman and Caleb. But they couldn't even chance that, could they, Marshal? They had to get rid of the kid!"

Matt rose. "I'll have a talk with Colt Coleman, Dan. Don't expect it'll do me much good. But I'm curious about Jon Riley. Coleman ought to know why Riley's come back gunning for him."

Dan's face was still set in the grip of futile anger. "Lot of people would like to know that," he muttered.

Matt hesitated, still bothered by the sheriff's killing. He couldn't link Riley and the sheep-

82

men to it, nor could he see where Spur fitted in, despite Dan's deep-felt conviction.

He remembered the two unaccounted-for men who had been at the bar when he and the lawyer, Pepper, had stopped in for a drink.

"What about this windbag attorney, Pepper? Whose side's he on, Dan?"

"Goldy Pepper?" Dan's mouth made a lop-sided O. "Harmless old coot. Used to be county attorney. Drank too much, talked too big and did little else. Old Coleman finally threw his political weight behind that shyster, Musick, and Pepper lost the next election." Dan made a weak gesture of disparagement. "I don't think Goldy likes Spur, if that's what you're after, Marshal. And he and Jon Riley were pretty friendly. Lived at the same boarding house and spouted poetry to each other. Pepper still lives there. Has a hole-in-the-wall office over Burke's coal and wood store, but spends most of his time in one of the bars on Main Street."

Matt nodded his thanks. "The sheriff's dead," he reminded Dan. "You still bitter about the law?"

Dan shrugged. "It's too late to tell Earl I misjudged him," he muttered. His eyes blinked as Matt tossed him a badge.

"I don't think Earl ever accepted your resignation," Matt said. "The star's yours, if you still want the job after you get back on your feet."

Dan didn't say anything to this. He waited until Vickers was at the door. Then, his voice a hoarse whisper, he added: "I forgot to tell you something you ought to know. I saw Jon Riley last night. He was coming out of Reverend Sharon's house."

Matt frowned. "Why would Riley want to see a minister?"

"Nothing about Riley makes sense," Dan said crossly. "But I heard Paul Sharon agree to ride out to see Ann Coleman first thing in the morning. You might try asking him, Marshal."

"I will," Matt replied. He made a gesture to the man in the bed.

"See you around."

-VIII-

Reverend Paul Sharon's housekeeper, a plain-faced, middle-aged woman with a severe hairdo, shook her head at Matt's question.

"The Reverend left early this morning. Drove his buggy. No, he didn't say. But I know he was going to visit with the Colemans at Spur Ranch."

She started to close the door, but Matt put his foot against it. "Was it because of Jon Riley?"

Her face showed no expression. "I wouldn't know that," she said coldly. "Mostly the Reverend just makes social calls at Spur. He has known the Colemans for years."

She started to close the door again, and this time Vickers took his foot away. He stood on the low stoop and put his hat on. Whatever it was Riley had told the minister, it had been important enough to send the man to Spur early.

It bothered Vickers, because he could make nothing out of it.

With the sheepmen ready to start a range war with Spur, what had Jon Riley wanted of Coleman's youngest daughter? It was a question, he reflected grimly, that would only be answered when he found out the reason Riley, an ex-schoolteacher and friend of the Colemans, had been run out of Peaceful Valley by Spur.

The sun was already high enough to lay a meager warmth over the muddy, rutted street. Matt shaped a cigaret and considered his next move. The two men he had come to see were dead, but his responsibility was not ended because of it.

He walked back to the main business block and found the livery where he had left the chestnut. In high spirits, the animal nuzzled him. Matt saddled him under the covert regard of a hostler shoveling manure out of the next stall. He asked directions to Spur, got them and rode out of the cluttered yard into the teeth of a rising wind.

Chimney smoke began to lie flat across the roofs, trailing southeast in a gray banner. Vickers cut across Main Street and was about to make for the north trail when he glimpsed a tall figure striding down the walk a block ahead of him.

Goldy Pepper, Matt reflected, walked as though he owned Gunsmoke. A big, imposing figure swinging his cane, his top hat made him stand out among the others on the walk. Pepper had a purposefulness in his stride; but he bowed and tipped his hat in an elaborate gesture to the ladies, and his booming voice as he welcomed the men held a jovial note. He passed in front of Charlie's Saloon and kept going, and Matt remembered that Dan had said that Pepper had been a good friend of Jon Riley's.

Possibly the old windbag might know why

Riley had risked his life to come into town last night to see the Reverend Sharon.

Matt pulled his high-spirited chestnut about and touched heels to the stud's flanks. He drew abreast of the lawyer just as Pepper was about to take the narrow outside flight of stairs to his office above Burke's Coal & Wood Store. Matt hailed him, and the big man turned, his cane held in his right hand as though he were ready to take issue with anyone who crossed him. When he saw Vickers, his whiskey-veined face cracked into a wide, friendly smile.

"Glad to see you again, friend." His voice was big, affable. "Let me buy you a drink—"

Matt shook his head. "Too early for me. Besides, isn't this your office?"

Pepper pointed up the flight of stairs with his cane. "That cubbyhole? I used to have a real office, over by the county building. Didn't really need it, though." His voice took on a casual, nonchalant quality, but Matt sensed an underlying bitterness in the man. "Don't often have clients with real money these days, Matt. You don't mind my calling you Matt, do you?"

"No." The marshal dismounted as Pepper talked and tied the chestnut to the short tie-bar. "Mind if I have a talk with you, Mr. Pepper?"

"Not at all, not at all, son," the lawyer boomed. He looked longingly down the street toward Charlie's Saloon. "Sure you don't want a drink?"

87

"Never drink this early in the morning," Matt assured him.

Pepper's florid face held disappointment. "Come on up, then." He started to ascend, his weight shaking the flimsy staircase. "Mighty bad business, Earl's killing." His voice was loud, but without any real sympathy. "Bad timing, too, with all this bad feeling between the sheepmen camped on the Longhorn and Spur."

He pushed his door open, stepped inside and made his way directly to a walnut cabinet. From a niche within he produced a bottle of bonded bourbon and two glasses. He poured a shot into one and held it up to the gray light seeping through his dirty windows.

"First of the day, Matt. Clears the cobwebs."

Matt was looking over the small office, the two stuffed chairs, a battered rolltop desk cluttered with papers. A walnut bookcase attracted his attention. There seemed to be only two or three titles concerned with law. Blackstone was there, alongside the Bard of Avon, a slim volume entitled *Omar Khayyam* and, strange bedfellow, Thomas Paine's *Liberty*.

Over all lay dust, which indicated to Vickers that H. Goldwyn Pepper did little to disturb it.

Pepper had finished his drink when Matt turned to him. The lawyer was eying Matt's badge with quizzical interest. "A lawman, Matt? You could have told me last night." His tone was accusing.

Matt ignored it. "You don't like Spur, do you, Mr. Pepper?"

The lawyer put his glass down. His eyes were watering. He took a handkerchief from his coat pocket and blew his nose.

"The Colemans and I, as the poets write, are scarcely soulmates," he stated. "Why did you ask?"

"I was hoping you might be able to help me."

"On behalf of the law," Pepper stated pompously, "I am always willing to help."

"Last night Jon Riley came to town," Matt went on, ignoring the man's interruption. "Milt Gavel and two hired gunhands rode in with him. While Gavel and the gunslingers waited for him in Charlie's Saloon, Riley went to see Reverend Sharon. This morning, bright and early, the Reverend drove to Spur. Does that mean anything to you?"

Pepper turned and reached for the bourbon again. This time he took it straight from the bottle.

"Riley was friendly with the sky pilot, Matt." His tone was noncommittal. "He probably just dropped by to say hello to Paul Sharon."

"Just to say hello?" Vickers' voice held a thin skepticism. "Last night Riley took a long chance coming to town. If he had run into Spur riders, it might have touched off more than he could handle. It was a nasty night, anyway. I don't see

Riley coming all the way from the Longhorn just on a social call, Pepper."

The lawyer sagged down into a stuffed chair. "Well, I don't know what to tell you, Marshal. I haven't seen Riley since he left the valley almost two years ago. Not many in town read more than the weekly paper. Riley lived across the hall from me, in Amy's, and we used to argue about the Knights of Labor and then switch to a comparison between a couple of new writers, Bret Harte and Sam Clemens. Many times around the breakfast table we—"

He leaned back, recollection of those days fading in him, leaving an odd regret in his face. "I don't know, Matt. The Jon Riley I knew was a schoolteacher—an educated man. I don't know what happened to change him. I don't have an idea in the world what he's got on his mind, except that he hates Spur."

He paused as footsteps sounded on the rickety stairs. The visitors didn't knock. They opened the door and walked in, and they seemed surprised to find Matt Vickers there. Matt looked them over. They were the same two hard-looking men who had been at the bar when Pepper had treated him last night.

The lawyer waved to them. "Sit down, boys. I'll be with you directly." He turned to Matt. "Couple of clients to see me about water rights down the valley."

Matt nodded in their direction. "Howdy." He picked up his hat. "Thanks for talking to me, Pepper." He shrugged. "Reckon I'll have to ride out and see Colt Coleman after all."

Pepper poured him a drink. "It's a long ride to Spur, Matt. And the weather isn't fit even for a sheepherder."

Matt hesitated. "Maybe you're right." He had the drink and went out.

The man from the United States marshal's office was on his way down the stairs when a burly, range-clad man turned away from the rack where he had just tied a hammer-headed grulla and started for the stairs. He was a blond man, in his thirties, barrel-chested and bulky, wearing a grease-stained Mackinaw coat. He lifted his head to Matt and came to a halt on the fifth step, blocking Vickers' descent. Mean gray eyes narrowed on Matt, and a sour look spread across his features.

Matt stopped two steps above the man. There was no give to this burly newcomer; he was in a mood for trouble.

Remembering the manhandling he had received in Jed's cabin, Matt felt the prod of a wicked anger shape his reactions. He said bleakly, "It's your move, mister."

The big man chuckled. "I see somebody worked you over already." His knuckle-scarred hand tightened on the railing as Matt's eyes narrowed. "Don't let that tin badge go to your head, Mac. You want by, squeeze over to the side."

Matt shrugged. He edged over and started to come down, and the other lunged for him, fingers reaching for a hold on Matt's coat.

Vickers' knee came up hard into the man's stomach, doubling him over. He brought his knee up again, into the heavy face, and the man went over backward, tumbling down the stairs.

Matt jumped down as the big man rolled over and shook his head like a dog coming out of water. He came to his feet, reached for his Colt and got it free just as Matt chopped down with his own drawn gun across the man's hairy wrist. The other dropped his Colt and grunted in pain. Vickers clipped him hard alongside the head.

The blond man fell across the tie-bar, and his dead weight snapped the dry pole. He rolled in an awkward heap under the chestnut's belly. The big stud stepped back, mincing skittishly, and a heavy shod hoof came down within an inch of the unconscious man's ear.

Matt holstered his gun and moved fast, dragging the man up onto the walk. He heard Pepper's door open and glanced up. The lawyer was on the landing, looking down, and his two clients were crowding the area behind him.

Matt waved. "We had words," he said thinly.

"Better come down for him, Pepper. I think he's another one of your clients."

He stepped over the unconscious man and paused briefly to inspect the brand of the grulla. *Spur!*

A hard anger pulsed in Vickers. The chestnut was skittish as he mounted, brought him around, and headed him down the street.

"Let's go calling on Spur," he muttered. "I want to see what makes that spread's riders so belligerent, men and women."

Pepper's two clients helped Big Sam Fisher to his feet after Vickers left. The powerful man shoved them back and braced himself on unsteady legs. He lifted an exploring hand to his cut lips and to the lump over his ear. He spat blood, and his tongue explored a couple of loose teeth.

One of the men who had helped him to his feet picked up the Colt he had dropped and handed it to him. Bald, wiry Hank Burke, owner of the coal and wood store, was looking through the window with glum interest.

He saw Sam Fisher shove aside the two men who had come down the stairs from Pepper's office. Sam evidently was not a man used to taking a physical beating and the two men quickly stepped back, leaving him alone.

Sam mounted the stairs. Pepper stepped aside to let him into the office. The "clients" came in behind Sam and gave him elbow room.

Pepper closed the door and whirled on the Big Spur ramrod. "You fool!" He shook his cane at the man. "I told you never to come to my office in broad daylight!"

Sam took it. He took it like some big dog recently beaten in an alley fight. He thrust his battered head into his coat collar and thrust out his swelling lower lip.

"Well," he muttered defensively, "ain't no need now to cover up—"

"I'll tell you when it isn't needed, Sam!" Pepper cut him off. "That was Matt Vickers you just tangled with! From the United States marshal's office in Tucson!"

Big Sam knuckled his unshaven jaw. "Pretty rough hombre," he admitted. He turned and headed for the filing cabinet. "I need a drink, Goldy—not a sermon. Shut up!"

Pepper reacted, but got a grip on his own temper. He knew how far he could push this bullheaded man, and when to ease up. "Serve yourself!" he snapped. He walked to the window overlooking the street and watched a man chase his hat across the freezing ruts. His manner was alert; the slackness was gone from his bloated face. His voice, when he turned to face them, was curt and direct.

"Listen close, Sam. We're going to have to change some plans—"

Sam tossed his drink down, then made a face as the bourbon burned the cuts inside his mouth. "Why? Earl's dead. Nobody's left to talk."

"There's Riley!" Pepper's tone was impatient. "This marshal's no fool, Sam. He'll nose around. And if he rides enough, he'll run into something."

"A lead slug between his eyes will settle that," Sam growled.

Pepper nodded. "If it's done right." He turned his regard to the stocky, acne-scarred man standing ill at ease by the bookcase. "If Guerney had done his job as well as I did mine last night, I wouldn't be worrying about Matt Vickers right now!"

Guerney made a defensive gesture. "Rain on the winder blurred things, Mr. Pepper—"

Big Sam cut in angrily. "Forget the excuses, Goldy! The boys at the hide-out are getting restless. They want a chance at the bright lights of town. Another week just hanging around up there, and they'll be shooting each other."

Pepper pointed his walking stick at Sam. "So they want something to do, do they? Maybe they'll have plenty to do, if this marshal gets wind of what we've been doing!"

"Vickers?" Sam's mouth twisted. "Aw, Goldy, I'll take care of him."

"You didn't make out so good just now!" Pepper jabbed.

Big Sam looked hard at Pepper, controlling his

95

anger with an effort. "All right. So I found out he's tough. They say there's a first time for every man. Mine was just now."

"Forget it," Pepper said. "I wasn't trying to prove anything." He moved away from the window. "Riley coming back gave us the break we wanted, Sam. But it can blow up in our face." He watched Sam try to think this out, then added: "Riley came to town last night. He went to see Paul Sharon. This morning the good Reverend drove out to Spur. You know what for?" He went on, not waiting for Sam to answer: "Because Jon Riley asked Sharon to see Ann Coleman for him. Because Riley wants to see Ann before he moves across the river."

"So?"

"You're not that thick, Sam," Pepper growled. "If she gets to Riley, there won't be a range war."

"Why wait?" Sam scowled. "Why don't we raid that sheep camp? Make them think Spur—"

"Milt Gavel's got twenty men out there," Pepper headed him off, "armed and itching to go. How long do you think a half-dozen men would last?"

"Goldy—you got any other ideas?"

Pepper walked to the bookcase and stood thinking. He looked at Sam. "You rode in from Spur this morning. Did you see Paul Sharon?"

"Said hello to him a few miles out of town."

Pepper nodded. "That means he's got one,

perhaps two hours start on you. Even if he gets to Ann right away and convinces her she should go to Riley, you can still intercept her if she leaves the spread. If she doesn't leave, she'll have to be watched night and day, Sam. If she gets to Riley, we're in trouble!"

"She won't go," Sam grunted. "Her sister watches her like a hawk. And her old man would have her hide—"

"Just the same," Pepper cut in, "we can't take that chance." He turned to the stocky man named Guerney. "You ride with Sam. You got a gun, and Spur is looking for gunhands. Sam'll hire you. That way one of you can always be around the spread."

"She won't go!" Sam snapped. "I know that girl, Goldy. She's scared of her own shadow."

"Maybe. But I hope she does." Pepper rubbed his nose with the silver head of his cane. "If she slips away, and you ride her down before she gets to that sheep camp—" He waited, grinning.

Sam's eyes widened. "I get you, Goldy." His laughter had an ugly sound. "Colt Coleman will break all records getting to Gavel's camp on the Longhorn!" His hand slid up and down his coat. "I'll be with them, Goldy—and I'll make sure nobody stops to palaver."

Pepper waved toward the bottle. "You and Guerney better kill it. You've got a cold ride ahead."

They killed it without further talk. Pepper stopped Guerney's partner at the door. "Wait, Lou. I want a word with you."

Sam Guerney went out, and Lou closed the door. He was a pale-eyed, silent man with a narrow dark face that seemed wrapped in brooding speculation. Lou Metz didn't talk much. But he was more dependable than Guerney, to Pepper's way of thinking. He should have sent Metz out to kill Vickers last night.

He voiced what he had in mind. "Guerney missed last night, Lou. Think you can handle the job?"

Lou didn't drink. He didn't smoke, either, but he liked the taste of tobacco. He usually kept a limp cigarette in a corner of his mouth.

"Marshal killing is risky," he said. "And this hombre is rough."

"Two hundred dollars worth the extra risk?"

"Make it five hundred."

Pepper hesitated. Then he nodded. "Five hundred. Get Vickers and come back here. You'll get the money then. You have my word on it."

Lou looked at the lawyer for a long hard moment. "Good enough," he murmured. Then he turned and left the office.

Pepper walked to the window and looked down on the cold, rutted street. His gaze lifted to the far slope of the valley where it met the gray-blue horizon.

Colt Coleman had owned Peaceful Valley for twenty years. But he had made some mistakes, and now they would cost him everything he had sweated for.

His first and biggest mistake had been kicking H. Goldwyn Pepper out of office. The second had been running Jon Riley out of the valley.

Pepper's eyes had a bitter, withdrawn look. He didn't give a tinker's dam for Riley and his problems. But Riley had come back with Milt Gavel in time to provide Pepper with the break of a lifetime.

With big Sam Fisher heading the tough crew in the back hills, they had been rustling Spur blind. Now the chance had come to smash Spur completely and take over what was left.

Only one person at Spur knew what they were doing. But Rita Coleman would never talk!

-IX-

The road to Spur was well marked. Riders and wagons had worn their grooves deep.

It was shortly before noon when Vickers came to the first loop of Copperhead Creek, which fed into the Longhorn a good eighteen miles north.

Spur was located within that loop, a rambling, split-log and stone ranch house which had changed little since Colt Coleman had designed and built it. An eight-foot pole fence, built stockade fashion, completely enclosed the main buildings. During the period of the Cheyenne raids, Spur had often stood alone, beating off the murderous attacks. Gray and weathered, it still bore some resemblance to a fort.

And the same watchful atmosphere seemed to prevail as a man with a carbine stepped into the open gateway, blocking Matt's entrance. The guard's gaze rested briefly on Matt's badge.

Vickers leaned forward. "I've come to see Colt Coleman."

"Who's talking?" There was a faint truculence in the Spur man's voice.

"Matt Vickers, United States deputy marshal."

The rifleman's manner changed. He nodded and stepped aside. "Mr. Coleman's in the big house.

Reverend Sharon's having dinner with him."

"I won't keep him long," Matt said. He rode on past the man into Spur's yard.

It was a good two hundred yards to the main house. A buggy was tied up at the rack. Matt rode by several buildings on his way to the house, and a half-dozen men, scattered throughout the sheds and bunkhouse, watched him. The thought came to Vickers that Spur was an armed camp, primed for trouble. Ordinarily, few hands would be found around the main spread at this hour, and even a big ranch like Spur would keep only a nucleus of working hands during the winter months.

But with trouble waiting across the Longhorn, Coleman was keeping a sizable force on hand.

Matt dismounted by the buggy and, turning, caught sight of the man walking toward him. Owen Sale's right hand was bandaged, but he held a cocked gun in his left.

Matt said: "Hold it, feller! I didn't come looking for trouble. I want a word with Mr. Coleman—"

Owen started to shake his head. "You got anything to say, I'll—"

"I'll take care of him, Owen!" the girl said. "Leave us alone!"

Matt turned to look at the girl in the doorway. Rita Coleman must have seen him coming through the window overlooking the deep veranda.

He smiled. "Thank you, Miss Coleman. I'm sorry if I'm interrupting your dinner. But I'd like to see your father."

Her manner was unfriendly. But in a housedress, Rita Coleman looked feminine and soft and strangely vulnerable. She was a beautiful girl, holding herself stiff and unattainable at home, riding arrogantly and tomboyishly in town.

"I didn't expect you'd come to see me," she answered sharply. "After yesterday, you are a fool to show your face here. One word from me, and my father would have you horsewhipped and thrown off the ranch."

"Not if you told him the truth," Matt said dryly. "And I believe you would." His smile was easy. "Besides, I apologize, Miss Coleman. I'm sorry about my display of temper. But I really came on other business. It concerns your father."

"I run Spur," Rita said. "If you have business concerning the ranch, speak to me about it."

He considered this. "I'd rather speak to your father," he repeated. "But if you insist, I'll tell you why I came to Spur. It concerns the matter of Jon Riley—"

He was quite surprised at the reaction of Rita Coleman. She flinched as though she had been struck and turned her face away from him, and it occurred to Matt that he had stumbled onto something sharp and hurtful to this girl. Jon Riley was a name not lightly mentioned here.

"Just a minute out there!" a voice rumbled. A stocky, grizzled figure in green wool shirt and tan corduroy trousers loomed up behind Rita. He was still holding a red-checked napkin in his hand, and there was a faint grease line around his mouth. He looked into Rita's white face and pushed past her, his eyes narrowing in sudden anger.

"Who is he, Rita? What's this hombre want?"

Rita's voice was strained. "I don't know, Dad. He says he has business with Spur."

Colt Coleman walked to the head of the stairs. He moved with some effort, his legs stiff, and leaned against the porch support. His eyes were bright, younger-looking than the rest of him, and alert.

"You looking for a job?"

"I've got a job," Matt said. He was aware of men coming up behind him, forming a semicircle at his back. More strongly than ever he got the feeling of an armed camp.

"You got a badge," Coleman conceded. "I can see it. What business have you got with me?"

"This is a friendly visit, Mr. Coleman," Matt replied. He paused as the old rancher winced and reached down to grip his left knee. Coleman obviously had been a thick-bodied, powerful man in his youth, but time had taken its toll of him. There had been too many nights sleeping out in the open, often chilled to the bone, seldom eating properly. His cheeks were furrowed with the gnawing pain of rheumatism, which had all but crippled him these last years. But his eyes retained their intense blueness, more startling because they studied Matt from under shaggy, snow-white brows.

"You're new in the valley." Coleman's voice was short. "Otherwise you'd know that when I want to see Earl or one of his deputies, I send for him."

"I don't work for Earl Wright," Matt said patiently. "That's one of the things I came to talk to you about—"

"If you're not working for the sheriff's office," Coleman interrupted rudely, "I don't want to talk to you." He started to turn to the door, but Matt's hard voice stopped him.

"I think you'd better hear me out, Mr. Coleman. I'm not from the sheriff's office, but Earl Wright did send for me. I'm a deputy United States marshal."

Coleman laid a long, puzzled glance on Matt. "Earl sent for *you?*"

Matt nodded. "He wrote there was trouble here, more trouble than he could handle."

"Ain't no trouble *Spur* can't handle!" Coleman snapped. "Earl's a fool. Next time I see him—"

"You'll see him at his funeral," Matt said. He felt his tone grow short, and he kept a hold on his rising temper. Coleman was a man used to having his own way, and he would see only what he wanted to.

"Earl's dead?"

"Someone shot him last night. Put a bullet in his deputy, too."

"Jon Riley!"

Matt shook his head. "Not Riley. Not anybody from that sheep camp on the Longhorn."

Coleman wadded his napkin in his fist. "You saying that someone from Spur shot the sheriff?"

"I ain't saying anything yet," Matt growled. "I'm not accusing anyone. I don't even know what the trouble is about. Not all of it, anyway. That's why I came to see you."

"You're wasting your time," Coleman said. "And spoiling my dinner—"

"Someone spoiled Sheriff Wright's dinner, too!" Matt could feel his anger, like a bad taste in his mouth. "Nobody seems to have thought much of him around here. A fence sitter. But he thought enough of his job to try to do something about the trouble you're trying to forget is waiting for you across the river. The kind of trouble—"

"Sheep!" Coleman snarled. "Just a bunch of mangy sheep! And I don't need an outsider sticking his nose in my affairs. Spur's handled its problems for better than twenty years—"

"Then it's time somebody helped you out," Matt cut in coldly. "This trouble isn't a bunch of young bucks off the reservation, Coleman, nor a rustler or two trying to make a few bucks the easy way." He stood still while Coleman spat deliberately to show his contempt.

"There's Milt Gavel and Jon Riley with eighteen or twenty men camped across the river. I heard that much from the sheriff. Whatever reasons they have, they must think they're good ones. You have yours. But I—"

"Sheepherders!" Coleman's voice held utter contempt. "Gavel's tried to cross the Longhorn before. I stopped him once—and I'll break him this time!"

"What about Jon Riley?"

He had expected a reaction, but he was surprised at the intensity of it. He saw Rita Coleman whirl and go into the house. Coleman's voice blasted at him. "I told Riley I'd kill him if he ever dared to come back to Peaceful Valley. I meant every word. If he crosses the river—"

There was a stir at Matt's back. Sam Fisher's hard voice broke in on Coleman.

"Riley already has, Colt!"

Matt edged around, hearing muttering from the men behind him. Coleman had straightened away from the railing, his eyes blazing.

Sam Fisher pushed through the group. He had dismounted and was leading his horse. He let the reins drop, and the grulla turned away, heading for the barn.

"Jon Riley rode into Gunsmoke last night, Colt.

106

Milt Gavel and a couple of gunslingers rode with him. I heard it all over town this morning."

Coleman turned to Matt. "You knew this?"

"I knew it," Matt conceded. "Riley didn't cause any trouble. He wasn't looking for a fight."

Coleman came the rest of the way down the steps. He stood close to Matt, a short, gnarled man fashioned by that hard country. "By Gawd!" he exploded. "If someone gunned Sheriff Wright, we know the polecats who did it! If Riley and Milt Gavel were in town, they killed Earl!"

"Riley didn't kill the sheriff. Neither did Gavel. Riley was in town on private business. That's why I rode out here. Riley rode nearly twenty miles in miserable weather to see Reverend Sharon. And this morning Sharon drove up here to see you. I want to know what Riley told Sharon that would bring the minister out here."

"I didn't even know Riley was in town last night," Coleman snarled. "If he had business with Paul Sharon, I don't know about it." He seemed baffled and angry. "Paul Sharon is an old friend of mine. Far as I know, he's out here on a social call."

"Let me speak to him for a few minutes," Matt suggested.

It rubbed Coleman the wrong way, and Matt knew it as soon as he had said it.

"You've interrupted my dinner," Coleman snapped. "I've got nothing more to say to you."

"Then let me speak to your other daughter, Ann—"

Coleman was turning away from him, and Matt didn't expect the blow. The old cattleman whirled around and back-handed Matt across the mouth. Vickers staggered back, and Big Sam came up and clubbed him behind the ear. Matt went down. He felt the cold earth press against his cheek, and his tongue probed the new cuts in his mouth.

"Coleman!"

The stern voice from the house made Coleman's decision for him. He shook his head at Sam and turned to look at the tall gaunt man in the black frock coat who had come to the door.

"This is nothing that concerns you, Paul."

"Violence always concerns me," the minister said.

Matt managed to get to his hands and knees. The blow had started a dull pounding in his head. He felt slightly sick. But the cold air blowing across the yard revived him. He started to get up, and Big Sam put his foot down on the small of his back, holding him.

"He came here looking for trouble, Colt." Sam's manner was ugly. "I wouldn't put too much stock in that badge, either, until we check him back in Tucson. I think he's a phony. He's a friend of that windbag, Goldy Pepper. And you know how thick Goldy and Jon Riley were!"

Coleman was still looking at Paul Sharon. He shrugged. "Let him up, Sam!"

Sam spat into the ground. He stepped back, and Matt came to his feet. He could feel blood on his chin. He brushed it away with the back of his hand.

Coleman made a motion to the men behind Matt. "Get him out of here! Don't ever let him ride through that gate again!"

There was nothing more Matt could say. Standing there, feeling the hostility of the men who were ringing him, he knew talk was useless. But he managed one bitter, meaningful statement before he turned to his cayuse.

"I'll be back, Coleman. I'll be back!"

Coleman's face was like fissured granite. "Get out!" He turned and mounted the stairs.

Matt stepped up into the chestnut's saddle and swung away. Big Sam was watching him, hand on his Colt butt, a lopsided grin on his split lips. Matt rode through the men, stiff-backed and angry, and out through Spur's gate.

He had gotten nowhere at Spur. But he knew now that there was more behind this trouble than sheep. And he had until Monday to find out what it was and try to head it off.

Rita Coleman was standing just inside the door, looking out through the window. She saw Matt mount and ride away, and she turned to the big round oak table where Ken and Ann still sat. Ken got up, dropped his napkin over his picked-over meal and left.

Ann's face had a stricken look, and Rita realized that her sister must have overheard what had taken place outside. She was a slim, ash-blonde girl with a tendency to be mousy in the presence of others. But her eyes on Rita were dark and accusing, and Rita, for once, lacked words to communicate with her sister. She ignored Mattie's question as she left the room.

Mattie, Coleman's Negro cook, stood in the kitchen doorway, surveying the remains of her well-planned meal. Ken's plate had barely been touched. Reverend Sharon's and Coleman's food was cold.

The gaunt minister walked into the dining room and stood looking at Ann, his manner uncomfortable and sad. He avoided the look on Mattie's face. She had been with the Colemans a long time—Ruth Coleman, Colt's wife, had hired her—and she was like one of the family.

Coleman clumped in and surveyed the deserted table. "Sorry this happened, Paul," he apologized. His manner was gruff. "Seems to have upset our dinner."

Sharon went for his coat and hat. "I think I'd better go—"

Coleman's brows beetled. "Why? Because of what happened out there?"

"Perhaps." The minister pulled on his fur-lined

gloves. "Maybe he has a right to know, Colt. A secret can fester in the dark, become malignant." He shook his head. "I've been your friend for twelve years. I watched your girls grow up in my church. Now I don't know them. I don't know what's happened to them—or to you. I don't even see you in church any more."

"You know what happened, Paul."

Paul Sharon looked at Ann. She was sitting with her head bowed, like a chastened small girl waiting to be released from the table.

"I think I do, Colt," he said. "But I still haven't found it in my heart to believe it of Jon Riley!"

Coleman sneered. He walked to the table and laid a heavy hand on Ann's shoulder. She winced and lifted her face. She was afraid of her father.

He said, "Tell him, Ann. You know what happened that night."

She turned her gaze to Paul Sharon. She seemed to shrink into herself; her eyes held a tortured appeal.

The minister said quickly: "You don't have to tell me anything, Ann."

She got up and started to leave. Coleman growled, "Wait! I didn't—"

But she didn't stop. Coleman took a step after her, shaking his fist. Then he stopped and turned back to Sharon.

"Maybe you'd better go, Paul!" His voice was thick, bitter.

Paul Sharon walked to the door. He paused to look back at the old man by the table, stooped and unrelenting.

"That marshal was right, Colt. Jon Riley came to see me last night. He hates you. But even so, he doesn't want trouble. He asked me to talk to Ann for him. He wants to see her."

Coleman's reply was stony, harsh. "Your buggy's waiting, Paul."

Sharon smiled forlornly. "Whatever happened that night, it's left its mark on you, on Ann and Rita, and—the Lord help us—on Jon Riley!"

"Not the Lord!" Coleman corrected him grimly. "What marks are on Jon Riley, I put there!"

Paul Sharon tried once more. "Let her go to him. Let Ann see Jon Riley."

"I'll see them dead first!"

Sharon's gaunt features showed shock. He let his hands fall by his sides. "The Lord have mercy on you," he muttered. He turned and went down the steps to his buggy and drove out of the yard.

Coleman followed as far as the door. The bitter wind blew inside, chilling the room. He saw the men in the yard, clustered in small, curious groups, eying the house. He didn't know half of these men; for more than a year now Rita had run the ranch, with the help of Sam Fisher.

He closed the door and turned back to the table. The food on his plate repelled him. He felt old and tired and cold—cold to the very marrow. He made a curt gesture to Mattie, standing crestfallen in the kitchen doorway.

"Clear it away—dump it somewhere." He stalked off to the fireplace and sank down in a chair facing the fire, feeling his years and bitterly resentful of them.

Ann Coleman lay across her bed, looking up at the rough oak beams exposed through the plaster ceiling. A lamp hung from a brass chain over the bed, and the reflector threw enough light for her to read by. But she wasn't reading. For the past year and a half she had spent long, empty hours in that room, trying to find answers in the rough-planed wood overhead.

She heard her door open and close and knew Rita had come in. She didn't turn or say anything.

Rita came to the foot of the bed and looked at her. It was cold in the room and very still. They heard Ken's door close, and a few moments later the back door banged shut. The sound faded into an aching loneliness that seemed to grip the big house.

Ann turned on the bed and looked up at her sister. Rita was standing by the carved bedpost, and her attitude was hostile.

"You want to go to him, don't you?"

Ann shook her head.

"He's waiting for you. He's out there across the

river, waiting for *you!*" There was bitterness in Rita's face, pinching it.

Ann's voice was small. "I'm not going."

"Why not? He came back. He said he would." Rita's hands clenched around the bedpost. "He thinks that much of you. He knows what awaits him if he crosses the river. But even so he's come back—"

Her voice broke, and Ann sat up, shocked at the grayness of her sister's face, the breakdown of this girl who was always so definite, so sure of herself; the sister she both dreaded and admired.

She was moved to pity. "Rita, I'll never see him again. I promised you that night. I'll never hurt you. I don't ever want to see Jon Riley again!"

"Go to him, Ann!"

Ann Coleman stiffened. "Go to him?" Her voice held bewilderment.

"He has a right to see you," Rita said. "Maybe you should hear what he has to say!"

Ann stared at her.

"You never gave him a chance!" her sister cried. "You fool, you never gave him a chance! If he had been mine, do you think I would have done what you did? Turned away from him?"

Ann stood up and clutched at her sister. She was smaller than Rita, frailer. But a shocked intensity gripped her; her fingers dug deep into Rita's arms.

"That night, Rita—that terrible night—when you said—"

"Go to him, you fool!" Rita tore herself away and slammed the door shut behind her. Ann stood stiffly by the bed, staring at the door, numbed by a horrible realization. Then reaction set in; she turned to the bed and buried her face in the counterpane and began to cry.

-X-

The wind shifted to the northeast, and with the change came the cold. It dropped twenty degrees in the next four hours. The sky changed, too. The high thin clouds which had filtered the sun thickened, and a winter grayness spread over the land.

Matt Vickers halted the chestnut by a thin cedar stand and dug in his bag for an old wool sweater. He put this under his coat and then worked gloves over his stiff fingers.

The stallion nosed around the base of the young cedars, cropping at something he found edible. Matt walked around, stamping circulation back into his legs. He studied the overcast sky. It could mean snow. But it was too cold and the wind was wrong—

He saw the rider, a passing glimpse, far away, moving quickly in behind a low hill. He put his attention on it, waiting. He was too old a hand at this game not to expect trouble. He was sticking his nose into something that more than one man had already been killed for; he wasn't fool enough to feel that the badge he wore gave him immunity.

He waited long enough for the rider, if he were on innocent business, to show himself. And the

116

thought came to him that the man might have been headed the other way.

He slapped at his shoulders to work warmth into his arms. The loneliness of this Arizona land, still largely unsettled, crept like the cold into his bones.

Even in Gunsmoke there was warmth tonight—and women. A man was a fool to ride single-hitched; Mary had been dead for ten years now.

The chestnut came up and nudged him, and he ran his hand over the steaming chest. "No percentage in it, Bill," he told the stud. "But a man's got to try. . . ."

He was thinking of Riley in the sheep camp on the Longhorn. He didn't expect too much of this day's visit.

He mounted and rode north by west, following a long narrow valley which threaded through stony hills. The grass was dead, and there had been little of it. He saw no signs of Spur beef, which surprised him, for he had been riding across Spur range since he had left the ranch.

He came down into a sandy wash and surprised a white-tailed buck drinking from a small, ice-rimmed pool. The buck whirled and went away from him. It topped a low ridge and almost instantly wheeled at an angle, leaving the impression in Matt that something just behind the dip of the ridge had startled him.

He thought of the rider he had seen, and alertness cloaked him. He headed up the wash, keeping clear of slopes that might provide cover for a rifleman. And looking over the land, he wondered what Milt Gavel wanted on this side of the Longhorn, what Milt and his brother had wanted five years ago. Sheep had a reputation of being able to grow fat on land that would starve a steer, but Matt doubted even sheep would find enough to eat here.

Still, a man had his own motives. Perhaps the enmity between Gavel and Coleman went further back and reached deeper than sheep. He could understand Milt Gavel. But he could not understand what drove Jon Riley.

He pushed the chestnut now, suddenly not relishing the thought of spending a bitter night in these hills. He came to the banks of the Longhorn before sundown, but the afternoon was gray and chill, and a bleak depression gripped him.

Across the river the ground sloped up to rocky ridges that seemed to merge into the granite shoulders of Squaw Peak. This, he had been told, was where Gavel ranged his sheep, in the narrow valleys off the southern slope of the mountain. But he saw no signs of the sheep camp, and he had to guess. He turned right and followed the course of the swift river as closely as the land permitted.

He heard the dog barking before he came to the ford. The sharp, crisp, staccato sound came from across the river and, pulling up, Matt spotted the dog running along the other bank. The river was wider here than at any point he had seen and shallow enough for him to see the riffle over the sand bars.

Matt leaned over his saddlehorn and searched the shadows across the river. He could see smoke rising above the jackpines, and he was about to hail the camp when the rifle whip-cracked in the silence.

The bullet made a slobbering sound as it hit a rock ten feet away and expended itself in the dying day. Matt sat very still, slowly lifted his hands and clasped them across his hat.

There was movement across the river now. A couple of men showed briefly on the edge of the pines. A gravelly voice he recognized called: "Who is it, Boyd?"

The rifleman on Matt's side of the river did not show himself. But he was close, up in the rocks behind the marshal.

"One man, Milt."

Gavel came into the clear, striding down to where the dog waited. He took a long look at Matt, then made a sign to the hidden rifleman.

He said to Vickers: "Come ahead, feller. But keep your hands where they are!"

Matt rode across the Longhorn. An icy wind

swept through the river canyon, and he wondered again what Jon Riley was after.

Milt Gavel had a shotgun thrust under his arm and kept his hands deep in his coat pockets. Behind him, two men holding rifles showed themselves briefly, then stepped back into the pine shadows.

Matt pulled up, and Gavel looked him over. The sheepman seemed more sure of himself here, less sullen. His brows arched slightly as he saw the badge pinned to Matt's coat.

"Wright get himself a new deputy?"

Matt shook his head. "Earl Wright's dead. He was killed last night. His deputy was shot, too. But he'll live."

Gavel cocked his head to one side, absorbing this bit of information. "Can't say I'm sorry," he said flatly. "Earl wasn't my kind of lawman."

"He didn't have to be anybody's kind of lawman," Matt said. "He did what he had to do."

Gavel wiped his lips with the back of his hand. "He's dead, you said. I won't argue with you about Earl." He pointed to Matt's badge. "You his replacement?"

"I'm Matt Vickers. United States marshal."

It caught Gavel by surprise and seemed to upset him. "United States marshal, eh? You could have said so last night."

"It might have helped," Matt admitted. He put his attention on the big collie that came up. The chestnut snorted warily, and the collie stopped and eyed the stallion.

"Go on back, Homer." Gavel waved toward the pines. "Go on."

The collie turned and padded back toward camp.

"Homer?" Matt's voice was curious.

"He's blind," Gavel said. His voice was short. "But he's Riley's dog and the best of the bunch. Riley named him after one of them Greek poets he's always reading."

"You read?"

"Not if I can help it." Milt chuckled. "So Spur figured they'd need help, eh?"

"Not Spur," Matt muttered. "The sheriff did. He was the man who wrote to headquarters for an investigator."

"Earl jumped when Coleman barked!" Gavel said harshly. "Don't tell me about Earl. If you say he sent for help, then Colt Coleman was behind it!"

"I don't think so," Matt said. He unlocked his fingers and started to bring his hands down slowly. "Mind if I take them down? Arms are getting cramped."

Gavel shrugged. "Keep them in front of you, in plain sight. I don't have to remind you that if you make one wrong move, a half-dozen guns will slap you out of the saddle."

"You don't have to," Matt said soberly. He

leaned on his forearms. "I didn't come looking for trouble."

Gavel didn't move. He didn't seem inclined to invite Matt over to camp; he preserved a faintly truculent, hostile attitude.

"It's mighty cold up here," Matt prodded.

"Right cold," Gavel agreed. Then, coldly: "Where do you stand, Marshal, in this trouble between me and Spur?"

"Right in the middle," Matt said.

"A bad place to be," Gavel observed. "A man stands to get shot at by both sides."

Matt shrugged. "The only place for me." He fumbled in his coat pocket for the makings, ignoring Gavel's scowl. "You planning to cross the river?"

"First thing Monday morning." Gavel's tone was final.

"The law will hold you responsible," Matt argued. His voice held no rancor. "These are wild times, Gavel. But even so, a man can't just move onto another man's land—"

"That's my land!" Gavel snapped. "Clear over to that ridge—" He pointed across the river.

Matt was surprised. "Not according to Coleman—"

"The devil with Coleman!"

Matt settled back in the saddle. He was still holding the sack of tobacco in his gloved hand, but he changed his mind about building a smoke.

"If you have anything to back up your claim," he said, "I'd like to hear it."

"I have. I had it with me when I tried to cross the river five years ago. A twenty-year lease, signed by Coleman himself." He shifted slightly, a sneer lifting the corner of his mouth. "You don't believe me, Marshal? I don't give a hang if you don't. But this is the way it was. Coleman needed cash, and my brother and I had some to loan. We needed more grazing land, and the country across the river was our answer. Not enough graze in most of it for cows, but sheep could get along. Coleman saw it our way at the time and signed the lease."

Gavel gave a short laugh. "Then came the war. My brother and I joined—the Missouri Regulars, Fifth Infantry. Coleman stayed put here. He was gonna hold onto what he had, he said. He didn't give a darn whether the slaves were freed or not. That's how he felt—"

Matt shifted in the saddle, turning away from the cut of the wind. The chestnut nickered impatiently.

"I'll make it short," Gavel snapped. "When me and my brother got back, we had to start clean. It took a while to build up our flocks. We didn't need the land we had leased, so we didn't bother Coleman. But five years ago we were ready. I rode over to Spur to tell Colt I was moving five thousand head of sheep across the river. He told me if I moved one single sheep across, he'd kill it—and the men who stood behind it."

Anger crept into Gavel as he talked, building up with his memories. "I reminded him about the lease he had signed. He told me where to shove it. Said it wasn't worth more than that, and that if I tried to take it to court he'd swear I had forged it. I knew he could make it stick. This is Spur country, Marshal. My brother was a hothead, and he talked me into making a move across the river anyway. We didn't have but two or three hands then, and some dogs. No gunhands. We crossed the river, and Spur smashed us. They did a good job. Bob was killed. Most of my sheep were run to death."

He took a harsh breath. "It's taken me five more years to get back here, Marshal. This time I've got guns behind me. I'm crossing the river Monday morning—and Spur ain't gonna stop me!"

"If you're telling the truth," Matt said, "I'll help you cross. And I'll see that Spur stays put. But I want you to stay here until I see Coleman again."

Milt's anger popped like a cork. "Like fun I will! Not for you, or for Spur! I promised Riley I'd wait until Monday. If I had my way, I'd be across now!"

Matt said tightly: "I'd like to speak to Riley."

Milt stepped back, his voice reluctant, still

angry. "He's back there. But he won't talk to you, Marshal. He's not talking to anybody today."

"All the same," Matt insisted, "I'd like to try."

Gavel hesitated, then nodded. "Unbuckle your gun belt and hand it over. Then get down. I'll take your cayuse."

They walked together toward the trees. Matt saw the fire beyond, glowing through the dusk. He sensed the men in the shadows, standing back, watching.

Gavel had draped Matt's gun belt over the chestnut's saddlehorn and was leading the animal. He stayed two paces behind Matt. They came up to the roaring fire where the bulk of Gavel's men were grouped: silent men, clustered in small, clannish groups.

Two chuck wagons bulked in the shadows ringing the fire, and the smell of strong coffee added a cheerful touch to the otherwise watchful atmosphere.

Gavel paused. "Riley's in that shack, back of the wagon." He pointed. "He's wound up tight, fella. Don't rile him."

Matt moved away. He cut around the chuck wagon and saw the shack in the darkness beyond. He made his way to the door and decided against knocking. Opening it, he stepped inside quickly and stood facing the tall man who had turned toward the door.

Riley had been waiting for someone. Matt saw

this in his tightly drawn face, and felt the sharp disappointment which crowded out anticipation. Riley's nostrils flared. He made a quick, dismissing gesture. "What do you want?"

Matt didn't answer right away. He was thinking that some men fitted in anywhere—like chameleons, they changed to fit their environment. But Riley wasn't that kind. In that dingy, crudely furnished shack, he stood out like a sore thumb. His white shirt, string tie, clean-shaven face and clean neck marked him. Yet Matt did not make the mistake of underrating the man. Jon Riley did not belong with this rough gun crew, but he was there, and he would hold up his end in the coming fight with Spur as well as any of them. Matt didn't doubt his capability with his holster gun—and he was aware that an intelligent man determined to kill was more dangerous than a dumb one.

In the moment he took to judge the man, he saw violence flare up in Riley. He raised a quick hand in a pacifying gesture.

"I'm Matt Vickers, United States marshal."

He saw the impression this made on Riley; a man grew up respecting law and order, and it was hard to forget. But Riley was strung too tightly to listen to reason.

"Fine!" he snapped. "I see your badge. And you've told me your name. You already know mine." He walked to the door, opened it. "If you've got something on your mind, talk to Milt about it."

Matt shook his head. "I've talked with him. I really came here to see you."

"I'm a bad conversationalist," Riley muttered. "I lost the stomach for it a long time ago."

"Eighteen months ago?"

Riley looked at him, a dark intensity flaring in his face. "Yes. Eighteen months ago."

"I won't bother you," Matt said. "But I just left Spur. I came here to talk to you. I want to know what happened between you and Spur that night. I—"

He didn't see Riley's hand move. But the muzzle that prodded him was hard and definite.

"Get out!"

Matt sucked in a harsh breath. "Don't be a fool, Riley! I'm the law. I've got a right to ask—"

"Get out!"

Matt edged backward. But he was bitter, too; he risked one more question. "You're waiting for Ann Coleman, aren't you?"

Riley's thumb clicked the hammer of his Colt back, and Matt's stomach knotted. Riley's face was gray. "Get out of this camp, Marshal! Go back to Coleman and tell him it didn't work! I'm crossing the river Monday morning! And we're riding through Spur—all the way through!"

Matt gritted his teeth. "I don't think so, Riley. I don't think you will!"

He turned and saw Gavel standing in the shadows, with the fire at his back. Milt had his shotgun cocked. Matt's chestnut was tied up by the chuck wagon.

Gavel said softly, "I heard you, Jon." He made a motion with the shotgun. "Marshal, you're not wanted here. Get on that cayuse and ride!"

Matt offered no argument. He walked past Gavel and climbed into the saddle. His cartridge belt and holster gun hung from the horn. He left it there.

Gavel walked with him to the river. It flowed dark and cold, and the hills beyond loomed up in the bitter night like shapeless, waiting animals.

Milt's voice held no anger. "I could have told you about Riley," he muttered. "But he'll wait, Marshal. He'll wait until Monday for her to show up." He made an oddly sympathetic gesture. "She won't come. But he'll keep waiting."

Matt said harshly, "Will it be worth it, Gavel? You lost your brother trying to cross this river five years ago. This time you've got the guns to make it. Will it be worth it? To you? To Riley?"

"Ask Coleman." Gavel's voice was bitter. "Ask him—and his daughter, Rita."

He stepped back, forestalling further conversation. "Turn right past the first hill, Marshal. You'll head down Copperhead Canyon. After eight, nine miles, you should run into a shack.

Travis' old place. Better than sleeping out in the open tonight."

Matt's voice was thin. "Thanks." He felt Gavel's eyes on him as he turned the big chestnut and sent it splashing across the cold, dark river.

-XI-

Matt took one look back when he reached the south bank of the Longhorn, but it was too dark to see if Gavel was still waiting at the edge of the river. The pines hid the campfire like a black, impenetrable curtain, and the rush of the river was a cold dismal thing in the night.

Matt let the chestnut pick its way southward. He hunched in the saddle, feeling frustrated and bitter; it was during moments like this that he felt like chucking the law. If the darn fools wanted to kill themselves, let them!

Yet the badge riding on his coat was more than a piece of metal and a ticket to a monthly salary. It was a way of life.

Somewhere in this violent tangle of human lives was the emotional thread which would help him unravel it. He had to reach some of the people involved. He had failed to get anywhere with Colt Coleman; and thinking back to the man, he knew it would be useless to see him again. Coleman was the old breed, tough, stubborn, single-minded men, great at opening up new country and sticking it out against the odds of weather and Indians and upset. But in human relations they were less than children; they had a narrow, selfish point of view that resisted change.

Gavel was remembering the first time he had tried to cross the Longhorn with his sheep. Maybe he did have a legal right to the range across the river. But it would take time to clear up the matter, and time was something Matt Vickers didn't have.

Jon Riley had shut him out. He was a bitter, hating man, and only one thing would stop Riley from crossing the Longhorn: Ann Coleman coming to him.

Matt didn't know why, or what was between Riley and Ann Coleman. Or Rita, for that matter. But he knew that Ann never left Spur, and he would have no chance to reach her now.

That left Rita. He would have to get to the bottom of this trouble through her. He'd have to see her again.

The chestnut blew noisily and stopped. Matt drew his thoughts from his problems and surveyed the night. The hills bulked like vague monsters, but off to the right he sensed a widening of the land. He hoped it was Copperhead Canyon.

He rode on, steadily getting colder. He felt numb now and dismounted several times to walk around and get some warmth back into himself.

On one of these times he heard the rider. From behind him, somewhere in the darkness, came the sharp ring of a shod hoof on stone! The wind was blowing his way, and he heard it clearly. The chestnut turned his head and snorted.

Matt went alert. Someone was following him. Had Milt Gavel sent a rider after him?

He mounted and rode off, following a tumbling stream he could hear, but not see, off to his right. Jed Sayer's shack had been located close to the Copperhead, he remembered.

He kept an ear cocked for the man behind him, but whoever he was, he wasn't risking coming too close at night. But it was obvious the man knew the country better than he did.

Matt sensed the house loom up even before the chestnut whinnied and picked up its pace. Wind rustled through the cedars lining the creek bed.

It was too dark to make out anything except that he was in a yard with what looked like a cabin ahead and a barn off to his right. He sensed the enclosure of a corral on his left.

It wasn't Jed Sayer's place, he felt instinctively. This was a bigger place. And it was deserted, cold and cheerless in the night.

Must be the Travis place, he thought. *Dan said it was up-valley from Jed's homestead.*

He pulled up in the yard before the cabin, and something warned him, sent a quick prickling down his back. He dismounted quickly, led the chestnut into the barn and heard a rustle as of a cat or mice, but nothing bigger. If Noel Travis had owned stock, they were no longer here.

He didn't chance a light. He stripped the saddle from the stallion and turned him loose, hoping the animal would find some feed. The barn, at least, afforded some protection from the wind.

He took his rifle and warbag and crossed the dark yard, skirting the horse trough. In the hills behind the spread, a coyote howled his displeasure to the cold bleak sky.

Matt put his hands on the latch, hesitating. Then he opened the door and went inside, slamming it shut behind him. He stood still in that pitch-black, unfamiliar room, trying to orient himself. A light was out of the question. The man outside was probably just waiting for a silhouette to show against the window.

He felt his way across the room, through an open door, into what he realized was a bedroom. His hands felt over the bed, and he took a blanket with him. He made a circle of the room, found no other opening and came back into the bigger room he had left. He kept on along the wall, feeling his way past a cupboard and then a range, and behind the range he found the back door.

He opened it very cautiously, making little sound, and found himself in the dubious shelter of a lean-to built against the back of the house. A pile of split logs loomed up in the darkness. He listened and heard nothing but the soughing of the icy wind among the brush beyond.

He closed the door quietly and went away from the house. Some fifty yards off, as nearly as he could judge, he felt the earth tilt upward. He scrambled up the slope and found a windbreak among two huge rocks.

He settled himself there. He couldn't see the house, but he felt certain the man who had followed him from the sheep camp didn't know he was there, either. He wrapped himself up in the blanket he had taken from the empty bed and propped his rifle by his head.

The rocks were cold, but the icy wind whistled over him. Matt Vickers eased down, using his warbag as a pillow, and prepared to spend an uncomfortable night.

He listened for a long time with the ears of a man trained to sound out the night, but he heard nothing except the lonely wail of the wind.

Finally he fell asleep.

Dawn came as a gray, cold smudge trailing across the eastern rim of the world. The wind died down.

Travis' old tomcat came out of the barn, stretched, yawned widely, and immediately froze in a crouched position as a catbird filtered down from the oak in the yard.

He waited with predatory patience while the catbird hopped about, pecking among old manure. Belly down, the tomcat inched forward, a foot at a time, freezing each time the catbird paused.

Daylight pushed the shadows back, and now

each detail of the small spread stood clear in the cold gray morning.

The catbird took three quick hops closer to the cat, then flicked its tail and took off. The tom turned an angry face toward the sound by the creek which had frightened the bird. Then he slunk around the corner of the barn to seek better hunting in the thickets beyond.

The shadow moved out of the cedars and came toward the house almost as quietly as the cat. Lou Metz was an old hand at tracking. He held his rifle across his waist, cocked and ready, and he walked easily, lifting his boots just above the ground, easing them forward.

The man he had followed from Gunsmoke was in Travis' house, probably still asleep. He saw no smoke rising from the stone chimney, and he didn't think the marshal had been fool enough to spend the night out in the open. Still, caution held Metz. Ahead of him lay a hundred yards of open ground, and if Vickers was up and waiting, he might find himself in a bad spot.

He moved swiftly now, coming in at an angle that would be visible from the one window facing the yard only if the marshal were looking for him. He reached the corner of the house and breathed easier, his breath showing white in the frosty air. Then, easing forward, he made one mistake; he stepped on an old zinnia stalk which made a loud crackling in the early morning stillness.

He froze, soundlessly cursing himself. He waited, edgy and uneasy, for the man inside to make a move. But the house *felt* empty!

His hand began to sweat, despite the cold. He could hear the stamping of a horse from the barn and he knew it was Vickers' big chestnut. Noel Travis' stock had been driven off more than a week ago.

It was possible that Vickers had decided to sleep in the barn. Waiting, and growing more unsure of himself, he had to face this possibility.

He slid his rifle down and rubbed his hands on his pants. He had slept little during the night, and his body was chilled to the marrow. A shiver went through him.

He had to draw his man out. He couldn't chance stumbling onto Vickers in the barn—he had seen the man draw against Owen Sale. He reached down and worked a stone loose. He straightened and cocked his arm and pitched it against the side of the barn.

He heard Vickers before the stone hit. Matt was on his side of the house and at an angle from him. The lawman said three harsh words: "Over here, fella!"

Metz whirled. He got off one quick shot with the rifle, and then Matt's bullet pinned him against the corner of the house. He braced himself and managed to work the lever, sliding another shell into firing position. He saw Matt just below the rock-strewn slope, walking toward him, a rifle held waist high. Metz brought his own muzzle up, his lips flattening against his white teeth with the effort. But he never got to pull the trigger. Matt's second shot doubled him—he fell face forward, away from the house.

Lou Metz was dead when Matt came to stand over him. Vickers studied the dark, thin features, recognizing this man as one of the two clients he had seen in Goldy Pepper's office.

The man must have trailed him from Gunsmoke. And this suggested another angle to the many-sided problem facing him. It made Matt take another mental look at the pompous figure of Gunsmoke's lawyer. Pepper and Riley had been friendly in the old days. And Pepper, like Riley and Milt Gavel, had cause to hate Colt Coleman.

Matt shook his head. He was too cold and tired to think clearly on the subject. Right now he needed a hot bath, a good meal and a few hours of unbroken sleep.

He started to walk away, then turned back to the dead man. He couldn't just leave Metz lying there, he thought wearily. But he doubted if the chestnut would take kindly to a double burden all the way back to town.

He went into the barn and saddled the stallion and rode out toward the creek. Metz's animal whinnied, and the sound guided Matt into a coulee a quarter of a mile beyond. The animal was picketed there, and Matt found the remains of Metz's cold camp. He smiled humorlessly at the knowledge that Metz had spent a miserable night, too.

He led the roan back to the house and packed the body across his saddle, lashing it securely. Then, with the roan on a lead rope, he cut away from the creek and headed directly for town, by-passing Jed's place, which he guessed lay somewhere behind the ridge forcing a bend in Copperhead Creek.

He rode steadily and reached Gunsmoke at noon. He left the body at Sam's place. Sam Wollek was pharmacist and veterinarian and coroner. And he also did all the burying for the valley. Matt left instructions with the man to check with him if anyone came to claim the body, or offered identifying information, and then went directly to the barbershop, where he soaked the cold from his bones in a hot tub. He dozed and woke only when Quito, the barber, looked in on him. The water had grown cold. He toweled and dressed, feeling relaxed and pleasantly tired.

Mrs. Lawson asked no questions. She cooked him three eggs, added two thick slices of ham and refilled his coffee cup twice. She made no comment as he left to go upstairs.

Matt locked his door, noticing that a new sash had been installed in his absence. He pulled down the shade, cutting off the weak sunlight, and after taking off his boots, crawled into bed. He fell asleep almost instantly.

Rita Coleman came out of the ranch house and walked across the yard to her buggy standing hitched by the barn. A Spur man helped pull a robe around her legs.

She drove out through the stockade gate a few moments before her father came out to the porch. Coleman hobbled to the head of the steps and stared bitterly across the yard. It was noon, and a weak sun poked fitfully through layers of clouds.

He leaned on his walking stick. His legs ached with a gnawing pain. He had slept badly and had heard Ann crying in her room, and this had not helped him.

Breakfast had been a dismal affair, and he had cursed Jon Riley and Reverend Sharon and, most of all, his crippling age. Ten years ago he would have handled the trouble across the river with a rough hand. Now he was unsure of himself, and of his men. And he could do nothing with Rita.

A strong-willed girl, she had run Spur for almost two years. She rode where she pleased and did as she wanted. But she was not happy, and because of that he hated Jon Riley with a deep and abiding feeling.

His bile came up and tasted sour, and he felt ugly. He went down the steps and across to the galley for a mug of hot coffee.

Big Sam Fisher watched Coleman go inside. He was saddling his horse, preparing to go to town. He saw Guerney come to the door of the bunkhouse and signaled to the man.

Guerney nodded. He sauntered over, and Sam said quietly, "Keep an eye peeled for the other Coleman girl. If she leaves the ranch, cut her off."

Guerney nodded. He stood curiously with his hands in his pockets as he watched Sam ride through the gate and head for town.

Owen Sale stood in the bunkhouse doorway and gently rubbed his bandaged hand. Behind him, on his bunk, Ira Cobb chewed morosely on a broom straw.

Sale didn't like Sam Fisher, and he was suspicious of the new man, Guerney. He didn't cotton to half the saddle tramps Sam had hired recently. But he remembered the men camped on the Longhorn and spat disconsolately.

"I wish we'd ride," he said, turning to Ira. "I'd like to get it over with!"

-XII-

H. Goldwyn Pepper paused in front of Sam's Pharmacy to light a cigar. He was an imposing figure, with a breath that smelled of bourbon from at least six feet away. He walked with a slight tilt, but now, as he puffed deeply on his cigar, he appeared benign and sure of himself. He bowed politely to a woman passerby before entering the shop.

Sam, a bald-headed, wiry man, was in a rear cubicle, mixing sedlitz powders. It was one of his stock remedies for stomachache, constipation, boils, and other ailments.

Young Freddy Jones, his clerk, was dusting the counters. He gave Pepper a cursory glance and announced in a loud, disrespectful voice: "Sam! Goldy's here!"

Sam came out, wiping his hands in his apron.

"Heard you have a customer for the back room," Goldy said. He sounded slightly curious.

"Yeah. But no one you can shake down for a drink," Sam said crossly. "Just some drifter I think I've seen around town before."

"I'd like a look at him, Sam. Might be a client of mine."

Sam shrugged. He turned and led the way into

an illy lighted room where Metz's body lay on a narrow bench covered by a sheet.

"That United States marshal brought him in," Sam said. "Didn't say what happened. But he asked me to tell him if anybody came in who could identify him."

Goldy lifted the corner of the sheet and looked down into Lou's dark, cold face. His teeth bit a little deeper into his cigar, but he kept his voice casual.

"By God, it is a client." He dropped the sheet and turned to Sam.

"Him a client?" Sam snorted in disbelief.

"Name's Lou Metz," Pepper said. "He and his partner came to my office yesterday. Wanted to hire me to look into their homestead title. Seems they were having trouble over water rights—"

Sam cut in hopefully, "I was going to have Mike dig a hole and bury him as is, Goldy. But if he's got property, perhaps his partner will want to pay for his funeral."

"I don't know about that," Goldy said quickly. "I turned them down. I didn't like the way they talked. But this gent left fifty dollars with me as an advance on my fee. You're welcome to it, Sam. Do what you can for him. If I see his partner again, I'll send him over."

He left Sam scratching his head. Outside, he let his feelings show on his face. He had trusted Lou Metz to do the job, but Vickers had proved to be

142

too good for Lou. And he knew the United States marshal would be looking for him soon, asking for an explanation.

He walked back toward his office and turned into Charlie's Saloon. If Matt was coming for him, this would be as good a place as any in town to see him.

He waited at the bar for the remainder of the afternoon. He bought a few drinks for acquaintances, but declined to sit in the poker games. During the interval he heard much discussion of the new marshal and a good deal of comment on the impending showdown between Spur and Milt Gavel and Riley. Judging from the conversation, the town was maintaining strict neutrality.

It was dark when Pepper finally left the saloon. The cold air blew some of the whiskey fumes from his head and cleared his thinking. He had been planning for months, and he was prepared to leave town on minimum notice.

He spotted Big Sam Fisher's bay horse tied up by the Lone Star rail and he wondered what had brought the Spur foreman back to town. Then he noticed the buggy at Caleb's rail across the street and knew that Rita Coleman was in town.

He walked quickly now, swinging his stick. He paused at the foot of the long flight of stairs to his office. The windows were dark; he had not been in since noon.

But he knew, the moment he turned the knob and stepped inside, that there was someone in the office. He closed the door and stood with his back to it, sensing the faint odor of perfume, of lilacs, in the stale air.

Harshly he said: "I told you never to come here!"

"How did you know?" Rita's voice was cool, from the darkness by the desk.

"I saw your buggy in front of Caleb's," he said. He moved away from the door, bent over the lamp. His face was heavy, jowls sagging, in the sudden glare.

He turned to face the girl seated in the over-stuffed chair. "I've no business with you," he said. "We quit being social years ago."

Rita Coleman stood up. The room was cold; she had on her coat and gloves, and her face had color. She had waited there a long time.

"I didn't come for a social visit." Her voice was aloof. "I'll make it short. I'm through, Goldy."

He ignored her. He walked heavily to the window and pulled the shade down, although the office was level with the flat dark roofs across the street.

The rebuff stiffened the Coleman girl. Anger laced her voice. "You don't believe me?"

He turned and looked at her, his manner demeaning. "No."

"You're a fool—a pompous, scheming fool!"

Her voice was bitter. "You think my pride won't let me! You've traded on it. I've let you and Sam have your way with Spur. But I'm through, Goldy."

He turned his back to her and went to the cabinet. Her voice rose harshly. "Ann's going to Riley! I'll see that she goes, even if I have to tell her the truth about that night!"

Goldy looked over his shoulder. The lumps on his heavy features seemed more pronounced tonight. He gave a short laugh. "You won't," he said. He made a motion to the chair. "But seeing you are here, be my guest. I have a bottle—"

"I don't drink!"

He took an almost empty bottle out and two glasses and placed them on top of the cabinet. He acted as though he hadn't heard her.

"You're through raiding Spur beef," Rita said. She said it calmly, firmly. "Take what you have. It ought to be more than enough to set you up in business elsewhere. More," she added harshly, "than enough payment for what my father did to your law career here."

He looked at her. "My, my, but you're generous tonight." He was mocking her and it brought blood to her face.

"I made a mistake—a terrible mistake," she flung at him. "And I've paid for it more than you'll ever know. I can't keep on paying. That's why I'm here, Goldy. I'm not going to let Spur

145

break itself against Riley and Gavel. I'm not going to hurt Ann any longer—"

"It's too late!" he told her. His voice was curt and uncompromising.

"No. Your threats won't stop me now. Take what you have and go. I'll give you until tomorrow. Then I'm telling Ann. And if I have to, I'll tell Dad!"

He considered this. It was a possibility he had contemplated; he had not given her credit for this much character. He nodded slowly. "All right. We'll stop raiding Spur beef." He didn't mean it, but he wanted time to think about it.

He watched her go out and stood for a long while, chewing on the soggy end of an unlighted cigar.

Matt Vickers had supper at the café and was on his way to see Pepper when Rita Coleman appeared on the rickety stairs. He was across the street and in the shadows, and he pulled back, surprised. He had not expected this.

Sam, the undertaker, had told him about Goldy, admitting that Pepper had claimed the dead man was one of his clients. But he had not reckoned the Coleman girl was one of Pepper's friends.

He watched her hurry down the dark street and went after her. He caught up with her on the corner.

"Need legal advice, Miss Coleman?"

She whirled. Panic showed in the outlines of her body. He moved closer, smiling. "I didn't know Goldy was that popular with the ladies."

He was half expecting her reaction, so he caught her wrist before her hand reached his face. "Sorry," he said at once. "I was being smart."

Her breathing was rapid. "I've nothing to say to you, Mr. Vickers!"

"But I have, to you," he replied.

She shivered. "It's too cold for street corner chatting. And I have a long drive back to the ranch. If you'll save this for some other time—"

He took her arm. "We can find a warmer spot, Miss Coleman. The café, perhaps. I'm curious. I'm interested in knowing why Spur, which opposed Goldy Pepper some years back, now has so much to do with him."

"Curiosity begets trouble," she said stiffly. She tried to pull away. "My business with Mr. Pepper has nothing to do with you. And I don't want to sit in the café with you. Now if you'll let me go—"

"Not until I get some answers!" His voice was blunt now. "I've heard about you. Very little of it is good. You're a headstrong girl who tries to run Spur and everyone connected with it."

"I boss Spur." There was a sharp arrogance in her tone.

"Then you'll be responsible, as much as Jon Riley, for what happens Monday."

She jerked free of him. "Jon Riley didn't have to come back. He could have stayed away." He felt the strain in her, the deep, hurt anguish.

"Why?" he pressed. "What did Jon Riley do to you, to your father, to make you turn against him?"

She caught hold of herself. "I don't know if it's any of your business!" she snapped. "That badge may have its privileges, Mr. Vickers, but it doesn't give you the right to pry into things best forgotten. Jon Riley deserved what he got that night. It's not for you to ask why."

"But it is," he answered sharply. "Jon Riley's waiting across the river. I saw him last night, a bitter, hating man. He was waiting for someone, Miss Coleman. Was it your sister?"

She shrank from him. He couldn't see her face clearly in the night, but he sensed her trembling.

"Didn't you ask him?"

"He wouldn't tell me. But it was your sister, wasn't it?"

"I don't know."

He pulled in a harsh breath. "Miss Coleman, I don't know why you hate Jon Riley, or what your father has against him. I can understand Spur's opposition to Milt Gavel. But Gavel won't move across the river until Jon Riley tells him. And I've got the feeling that your sister can stop Riley."

She didn't answer, and her silence was an affirmation. He pressed her. "I saw the men

148

Gavel's got with him. I saw the guns at Spur. You can't win. Believe me, when Gavel moves across the Longhorn this time, Spur won't stop him! Is that what you and your father want? Do you want to smash Spur?"

"I don't care!" All the bitterness and frustration of a mixed-up girl was in her outcry. "I don't care what happens any more!"

He heard boots slap the plank walk behind him, and he stepped back from the girl and partially turned. A man moved out of the deeper shadows, a big, hulking figure. He was holding a gun in his fist, and the muzzle caught a stray beam of light and reflected it.

"Move away, Rita!" Sam said. His voice was pitched low. But the intensity in the Spur foreman's voice shocked the girl.

"Get out of line!" he repeated harshly. "I'm going to kill him."

"Sam—*no!*" She moved quickly, stepping in front of Matt, between the marshal and the Spur ramrod.

Sam stopped. He was a dark, thick figure in the night, and the girl sensed his gathering determination to override her. The wind moaned around the eaves, and in the night a wagon rolled over the hard rutted earth, a lonely and dismal sound in the cold.

"Sam, you'll have to kill me, too!"

Fisher sucked in a baffled breath. "You fool! I

could have gotten rid of him. He was molesting you—"

"Take me home!"

Sam didn't move. She walked to him determinedly. "Take me home, Sam. Let him be."

Sam looked over her shoulder at Vickers. "Some other time, then, Marshal. Some other time, in some other place, when there won't be a woman to stand in front of you!"

Matt said, dry-lipped: "Some other time, Sam," and watched Sam move back, the girl with him; watched them turn and go out of sight around the far corner. Only then did he relax, and he was surprised to feel a cold sweat on his face.

It had been close. And he had Rita Coleman to thank for saving his life.

A cold windy corner in a strange town, he thought bleakly. *Some day it'll happen. You go looking for answers, and you find trouble!*

It was a dark and violent land, with the deep scars of a bloody war behind it and a violent breed of men swaggering across it. He took a deep breath and remembered that he had been on his way to see Goldy Pepper.

He turned and went back up the dark, windy street.

-XIII-

H. Goldwyn Pepper's light was still on, showing around the ragged edges of his drawn shade. The shop below was dark, and somewhere a baby started coughing as though it had the croup.

Matt saw the light in Goldy's window snap off as he started up the stairs. He hesitated, then decided to go on up anyway. He was on the fifth step when the door above him opened. The landing creaked, and the stairway quivered as Pepper came out.

Matt stopped. He rested his left hand on the railing and lifted his right to the butt of his holstered Colt.

Pepper's bulk was thick in the shadows above him. He didn't move.

Matt called, "It's me, Goldy. Matt Vickers. I want a word with you."

The shadow remained silent. Matt's stomach muscles knotted; he started to slide his Colt free.

Then Goldy's booming voice broke the silence. "You startled me, Marshal. Sure, come on up. I was just stepping out for a snort and a bit of socializing." His chuckle lay heavy on the cold air. "Don't like to drink alone, Matt. Bad habit for a man to get into."

Matt climbed the stairs. Pepper was already

inside the office, moving about in the darkened room. Matt closed the door just as the lawyer struck a match and lighted the still warm wick.

Pepper turned slowly, a big man with a pleasant smiling face, and waved Matt to a chair. "Glad to see you back in town, Marshal. After that run-in you had with Spur's *segundo* on my steps, I was afraid of what you'd run into at Coleman's spread."

"I didn't spend much time at Spur," Matt said.

"Oh? Been out riding? In this weather?"

"I've been riding," Matt admitted. He sat on the arm of the chair, one hand thrust deep inside his coat pocket. He decided not to mince words with this man.

"I thought you and Spur parted company a long time ago," he said. "The way you told it, you hated Spur, the Colemans in particular."

"You'll hear it from me again," Pepper said. He stood near the cold stove, his hat tilted back on his shock of gray hair, his whiskey-mottled face stamped with cold indignation. "I have no use for Spur and the Colemans—"

"I heard you!" Matt cut in. "But yesterday Sam Fisher was coming up here to see you. And tonight Rita Coleman came."

Pepper laughed. "Glad to find you that observant, Marshal. Now do you want to know why they came up?"

Matt fished in his pockets for the makings.

Goldy stepped to his desk, picked up a box of panatellas and held it out to Matt, who changed his mind about a cigaret.

"I'm waiting," he said, as Goldy produced a match and lighted the cigar for him.

"Big Sam Fisher came up to threaten me," the lawyer said. "After the way you manhandled him, he wasn't in a very convincing mood. And with a couple of witnesses in my office, he didn't push it."

"Threaten you?"

"Yes. Everybody in town knows I was Jon Riley's friend. Big Sam thinks I had something to do with getting Riley back here."

Matt nodded. "Makes sense." He sucked in smoke and blew it out slowly. "Rita Coleman figure the same way?"

Pepper said: "About the same. Only she didn't come to threaten me. She came to buy me out."

Matt's eyebrows raised. "Bribery?"

Pepper shrugged. "She thinks I know what happened to Riley. She offered me five thousand dollars if I'd leave town—leave the territory."

Matt got to his feet. "Jon Riley must have turned Spur inside out that night," he muttered. He walked closer to the stove. "Pepper," he said bluntly, "there's a dead man in Sam's back room. Sam tells me you knew him. He was a client of yours."

"He and Guerney," Pepper admitted. "You were in my office when they walked in yesterday."

"What do you know about them?"

"Not too much. Lou Metz—the man in Sam's back room—wanted me to go to the country seat to look into water rights on his place. He and his partner, Guerney, claimed to have a spread about thirty miles south of here. Said they were having legal trouble with some big outfit and wanted proof of a clear title."

"And they came all the way to Gunsmoke to hire you?"

Pepper drew himself up. "I have a pretty good reputation as an attorney, young man!"

"You never saw them before? Don't know anything about them?"

"I don't question my clients," Pepper snapped. "I'm not concerned with their backgrounds—"

"You should be!" Matt cut him off. "This Lou Metz trailed me to Gavel's sheep camp last night. Early this morning he tried to kill me. You know why he did this?"

Pepper looked flabbergasted. "Hanged if I know, Marshal. You sure *you* didn't run into him and his partner before? On some other business?"

"That's possible." Matt had to admit it was. He looked at Goldy and found it difficult to think of this big, lard-fat buddy of John Barleycorn as anything but what he appeared to be: a down-at-the-heels back-country lawyer, whose ambitions ran no further than enough business to keep him in liquor.

"Is Metz's partner still in town?"

"I haven't seen either of them since they walked out of my office," Pepper replied. He scratched behind his left ear with the point of his cane. "They left together, right after Big Sam walked out."

Matt frowned. "There's one thing bothering me, Pepper. Someone killed the sheriff because he was going to tell me about Riley. It wasn't Riley and it wasn't Milt Gavel, or any of their riders. And it couldn't have been anyone who worked for Spur. Dan told me Earl was Coleman's man."

"Coleman put Earl in office," Pepper agreed. "And Coleman could have taken that badge away from Earl at the next election. But Earl was nobody's fool, despite Dan's opinion, Marshal. It's possible he was fed up with Spur and saw a chance to make a break with Coleman when you showed up here. I wouldn't count Spur out if I were you, Marshal."

Matt nodded. "That's the worst part of it," he said. "I can't rule out anyone. Not even you, Pepper."

Pepper stopped scratching behind his ear. He stood very still for a moment, a thoughtful man considering Matt's remark. Then he made a gesture of agreement.

"That's your privilege," he said. "I'll tell you

right now that I didn't think much of Earl. But I learned long ago that I wasn't big enough to buck Coleman. So I took a seat on the sidelines and waited for someone else to buck him. Earl wore a star on his coat and was drawing pay for it, but in a way he was like me—he wanted to stay on the sidelines, too, and let his young deputy do the dirty work. We were two spectators to what was happening here—and I, for one, didn't give a hoot where Earl sat!"

"That's a long-winded way of saying I'm a fool," Matt said, smiling. "And maybe you're right." He started to move for the door.

Pepper leaned back against his desk. He seemed old and a trifle condescending, the way an old man is sometimes with youth. "Seems like you've run up against a stone wall here, Marshal. Riley and Gavel are going to cross the river, and nothing that you can do now will stop them."

Matt showed him a wintry smile. "It's still two days until Monday. Don't bet on it."

Matt had slept all afternoon, and now he wasn't tired. He had a couple of drinks in Charlie's and sat in a poker game. But his mind wasn't on cards, and he lost five dollars which he could ill afford. A marshal's pay didn't give him much leeway. Still, he had never been interested in making big money, and sometimes, when he felt low, he wasn't sure what he wanted out of life.

Take right now.

He wasn't getting anywhere here. Monday morning Riley and Gavel would move across the Longhorn, and Coleman would come out with his hired guns to stop them. And it was no longer a question of who was right; it was a matter of hate and pride and things buried deep.

Men would be killed, and nothing would be settled. After the killings the violence would smolder, to break out again later.

He felt like forgetting the whole thing. But Matt was a stubborn man. He went back over the people involved and remembered he had forgotten Reverend Sharon. He tossed in his poker hand and left the bar.

Paul Sharon's housekeeper faced him with her usual animosity. "He isn't here." Then, noticing the badge on his coat, her tone relented. "You'll find him in church. He said he had something to do there."

The church was a small white clapboard building a short distance from town, set in a pecan grove. It was used as a school six days a week. Reverend Sharon preached there on Sundays.

Matt walked up the lane used by the valley children. He could see a dim light flickering against the windows, and he paused by the door and looked through the nearest pane. Sharon was standing behind the lectern, his face buried in his hands.

Matt hesitated. *Every man carries his burden of trouble,* he thought. But he opened the door and went inside.

Paul Sharon lifted his head. Coming toward him, Matt saw that a Bible was open on the lectern.

The minister turned slightly to face Matt, and Vickers saw the torment on the tired face and knew that whatever was troubling this man had not been eased. Something like apprehension flitted across Sharon's face.

Matt said: "I've got to know, Reverend." His voice was gentle. "You know I have to."

Paul Sharon tried to evade him. "I don't know what you mean, Mr.—"

"Matt Vickers, United States marshal."

Sharon sighed. "All right, Marshal. What do you want from me?"

"You were at the Coleman ranch yesterday. You were there when I arrived. I wanted to talk with Coleman about his trouble with Jon Riley. I wanted to have a word with Ann Coleman."

It was cold in the cheerless, empty schoolhouse. But Sharon brought out a handkerchief and mopped his brow.

"I was there. But I still don't know what you want of me."

"Let me explain," Matt said. "Jon Riley is the

key to the trouble here. He can stop Gavel from crossing if he wants to. He can start or stop this bloody war that will almost surely break out Monday!"

Sharon avoided his gaze. He was a tortured man, bowed by his sense of failure.

"Jon Riley came to town to see you two days ago. Right after his visit you drove to Spur—"

"And you feel there is a connection? Something you, as a lawman, should know?"

"Yes."

Sharon shook his head. "I can't tell you, Marshal. On this Bible I swore that I would never tell."

Vickers' lips tightened. "I don't have to keep reminding you of what's going to happen Monday. As a man of God, is it more important that you keep silent?"

Sharon had fought this problem before Matt presented it to him; fought it and made his decision. He bowed his head.

"I've done what I could to stop it, Marshal. Believe me, I can do no more."

"Tell me what happened to Jon Riley at Spur. I'll take it from there."

Paul Sharon turned his face to him. The shadows were black on his deep-lined features.

"I can't tell you! I've done all I can. Now it's up to the Lord—" He dropped his hands by his sides. "On my word, I don't know what happened to Jon Riley that night!"

Vickers made a gesture of resignation. His voice was bitter. "Sometimes I wish I could do the same, Reverend: just say it's up to the Lord. But this badge carries an obligation with it that pinches my conscience. I've got to keep trying. I couldn't live with myself if I didn't!"

-XIV-

They buried Earl Wright in the morning. It was a bleak, windy day with a leaden overcast, and a brittle snow came whipping across the cemetery before the ceremony was finished.

A sizable gathering paid their last respects to the sheriff. But no one was present from Spur, nor did anyone from Gavel's sheep camp show up.

Paul Sharon stood at the head of the grave and read the services. Earl's widow was by his side; her two children, ten and eleven, were standing a few feet away with her sister. Mrs. Wright had had time to cry her grief out. She stood red-eyed and watched them lower the coffin into the pit while Paul Sharon read the final words.

The minister's voice was halting and as dry as dust.

Matt Vickers stood through most of it. From where he stood he could look across the valley to the foothills humping along the line of Copperhead Creek, clear to the massive bulk of Squaw Peak, its snow line lower down than the last time he had noticed it.

Lawyer Pepper was there, standing somewhat apart from the others, his gray head bared to the icy wind.

In a far corner of the cemetery two workmen were digging another hole in which Lou Metz was to be buried later.

Matt left before the end. He stopped at Charlie's for a drink and then went to look in on Dan O'Malley. The deputy was sitting by the window, a blanket wrapped around him, and Matt observed that Dan had a clear view of the funeral from his chair.

The deputy was in a depressed mood. "They got Earl. They got Jed and Noel Travis. And maybe they've even killed the kid!" His teeth gritted in futile anger. "If I could get out of this room I'd kill Sam Fisher! So help me, Marshal! I don't care what Rita Coleman testified to. Big Sam killed Noel Travis! And it was Sam, or his friends, who kidnapped Buzz Travis."

Dan's bitter monologue struck Matt forcibly. He remembered the body he had laid out in Jed's shack, the man Dan had said must be Ben Cavanaugh.

He had left Cavanaugh's body in the cabin, expecting that the sheriff would send a wagon out for it. The events following Earl's death had driven all thoughts of this man from his mind until Dan's bitter tirade had reminded him.

He put on his hat, and Dan turned to look at him. "Leaving?"

Matt nodded. "Something I forgot to do. I'll be back by night." He paused at the door. "Heard

162

talk around town. You might be Gunsmoke's new sheriff. That is, if you don't go around insulting everybody before election day."

Dan snarled, "I'll insult them all, if it means I have to knuckle down to Coleman to get it!"

Matt grinned. "Reckon you'll make a good sheriff, Dan—the hard way!"

He rode out of town a half-hour later. The wind was in his face, and the snow squall caught him as he turned up the small river valley of the Copperhead.

He pushed the chestnut. The country became familiar, and he knew he was getting close to Jed's spread.

Suddenly he turned and glanced back toward the low hills flanking the creek. And with the motion came wonder as to why he had done so. The faint prickling at the back of his neck warned him. Someone was on his trail! Matt had followed too many trails of his own; he had developed an animal sense concerning this. He saw nothing move in the broken country behind him, but the thought occurred to him that Metz's partner might have followed him out of town.

What had worked against Lou might work with the man behind him. It was worth a try.

He nudged the chestnut into a lope toward the bend in the creek and made the crossing at the same point as when he had first come to Jed's place. He didn't look back again. Jed's cabin came into sight as he broke through the thin willow screen.

The place had the same abandoned look as before. But Matt noticed immediately that the spring wagon was gone. And the thought came to him that the team would hardly have waited there all this time.

He dismounted and tied the chestnut to the corral bars. He forced himself to act normally, like a man not expecting trouble.

He was listening for some tangible evidence that someone was behind him—the faint ring of a shod hoof, the faint snort of a tired animal. He heard nothing but the wind in the brush.

He kept his walk easy, although his shoulder blades had the tightness of a man expecting a bullet to smash into them. He pulled the cabin door closed behind him and then moved fast.

He had a moment, in passing, to notice that Ben Cavanaugh's body was gone. The shack was empty, but the stove was warm as he brushed against it, although the fire in it had gone out.

Matt reached the rear window. There was no back door; only this small window looking out over a weed-grown area and the brush-covered slope that went up gradually toward a crumbly granite ridge. Four sixpenny nails driven into the framing around the sash and bent inward held the window in place. With his pocket knife, Matt turned the nails back and pulled the sash free.

It was a tight squeeze to get his shoulders through; the rest of him followed easily. He landed on his hands and the back of his neck and rolled to his feet. He had his Colt in his fist as he made for the brush on the slope.

It took him fifteen minutes of slow, careful stalking before he heard the animal cropping at spiky growth. A grin touched his lips. He cocked his gun hammer, crawled between two boulders and came to a gully shielded by buckbrush.

The animal he heard was below him, in the gully, about thirty feet away. It was a big mule, with a patchy gray hide, and it cropped unconcernedly.

Matt settled back, his eyes searching the brush beyond. He could see the front of Jed's shack from there, but he felt uneasy. Whoever had trailed him on the mule should be holed up within sight of the cabin, as he was, waiting for Matt to come out.

He started to move along the edge of the gully when a voice stopped him. It was dry and insolent.

"Purty good for a tenderfoot, fella. But a Comanche'd had your scalp the minute you dropped through the winder!"

Matt whirled. He had his Colt cocked and ready, but he'd never felt more foolish in his life. He didn't see anyone.

The voice came again, from behind brush-covered rocks on the slope. "Hold it, mister! I ain't after your hide! If I was, you'd never have gotten this far!"

Matt lowered his Colt. A small ragged figure that had been hunched up behind the rocks came toward him. He carried a Sharps rifle, and there was a twinkle in his eyes. He was at least sixty, spry as a wild rooster and stringy as an old goat.

He chuckled as he approached the marshal. "Fancy bit of stalkin', fella. But I had yuh covered with ol' Betsy here all the way. Lucky fer you I spotted that badge on your coat right off."

Matt cut in grimly, "Who are you?"

"Me? I'm Jed Sayer. Fella what owns this shack."

Matt Vickers shook his head. He sat down on a rock and ran a hand across his eyes.

"You're dead." He kept a straight face. "They've got you buried in Gunsmoke's Boot Hill."

Jed chuckled. "Then I'm Jed's ghost." His keen gaze surveyed Matt. "You the United States marshal they sent down here to look me up?"

Somehow the sly humor of the old codger convinced Matt. "Yeah. I'm Matt Vickers."

The oldster's bushy brows came together. "Heard of you. Glad they sent somebody with

166

sense." He stuck out a horny hand. "Was getting mighty impatient, waiting. But I reckon we can start right off—"

Matt took Jed's hand. There was nothing soft about the older man's grip.

"Whoa!" he said. "Before we start, let me get straightened out here. If you're Jed Sayer, then whose body is buried in Gunsmoke?"

Jed squatted down on his heels. He set the Sharps down by his side and reached inside his coat pocket for a hunk of chewing tobacco; he made an ineffectual attempt to wipe the lint and specks from it and took a bite.

His voice blurred as he talked. "Don't know his name, Matt. Some jasper who came Injunin' around the shack one day. Wasn't the first time I'd been shot at, so I was kinda expectin' trouble. He climbed into the corral where I keep Vittorio, my mule, an' I shot him plumb between the horns." He grinned at the memory. "Shot got Vittorio riled—he made a mess of what was left of the bushwhacker."

Matt hunkered down across from the old man and reached for his sack of tobacco. The wind blew cold across the creek, and the sky was blue-black. Another snow squall was in the making.

"About that time Noel Travis showed up—" Jed continued. "Me an' Noel were neighbors— his cabin's over there, behind that ridge."

Matt cupped his hands around his match and got his cigaret going.

"I knew them varmints would keep after me," Jed said. "So I told Noel to haul that body into town an' tell the sheriff it was me. Didn't know if we could get away with it, but that muttonhead we got for a sheriff went along with the story—" He paused to loose a brown streak of tobacco into the gully. "I faded into the hills an' snuck down to Travis' shack one night an' gave him a note to mail to Tucson."

Matt said: "Sheriff Wright's dead. Someone shot him two nights ago."

Jed was indifferent to the news. "Knew he'd get it sooner or later," he muttered. "He was afraid to move, an' a jasper who sits still when there's trouble is the one that gets shot."

He eyed Matt quizzically. "You run into his deppity yet?"

Matt nodded. "Dan's in bed, shot through the chest. Same man who killed the sheriff shot him."

Jed ran his fingers through his beard stubble. "You got any ideas who done it?"

"Some I'm going to work on," Matt answered levelly. "What do you know about the trouble here?"

Jed spit toward the gully again. "Sheepmen against Spur—that's the play, while the varmints in them back hills steal Coleman blind!"

"Rustling?"

Jed nodded. "Spur's own ramrod is behind it. Sam Fisher. A mean hombre with a fast gun hand. They been using this valley to run beef to a hide-out canyon in them hills. That's why they tried to kill me. Sam Fisher killed Noel Travis for the same reason. Me an' Travis was the only settlers near enough to spot 'em moving Spur beef. Getting rid of us gave them a clear run into the hills."

Matt straightened, dropped his cigaret and ground it under his heel. "I dropped in on you two days ago. Ran into two hardcases and Travis' boy in your shack." He recounted what had happened.

Jed grunted. "I was on my way back from trailin' them to their hide-out. I spotted Brazos an' the other one with Noel's boy, headin' for the canyon. I cut back an' follered 'em until I was sure where they was headed. Must have missed you in the meantime. When I got back I found Ben's body in the shack, on my bunk."

"Where is he now?"

Jed waved up the slope. "Buried him."

Matt rubbed the palms of his hands down his pants legs. His voice was steady. "Think you can find your way back to that canyon, Jed?"

The old Indian fighter snorted. He picked up his Sharps and gave a short whistle.

The mule lifted its head and came back along the gully to a point just below them.

"Ain't as fancy as that big chestnut you're ridin'," Jed growled. "But Vittorio takes me where I want to go. An' he's got more savvy than any cayuse an' most gents I've met."

-XV-

Ann Coleman came to the door of her room and glanced at Ken, who nodded encouragement. It was Sunday morning and the house was quiet, except for Mattie stirring in the kitchen.

Ken was in the hallway; he came back to Ann's room, his face flushed with excitement. "Hurry. Dad's still asleep. But Rita is up. She just went back to her room."

Ann hurried. She was dressed for riding, and there was a high color in her cheeks and a determined look on her face that changed her. She and Ken were much alike, but Ken had always had a more rebellious streak in him.

"I've got Baldy saddled and waiting for you by the back door," he whispered. "A few boys are up, but they're in the galley, giving Gonzales a hard time. They won't notice you."

Ann took the note she had scribbled last night and handed it to her brother. "Will you see that Rita gets this?"

He nodded. "I'll tell her after you've gone, sis. Dad, too."

He went with her to the back door. She was carrying a small bag containing a few cherished possessions, personal items. It was a cheerless Sunday morning, bleak and raw. The wind cut across the yard. Gonzales was already up, and his galley fires whipped smoke over the sheds. A couple of old-timers, not used to sleeping late, were having coffee. No one paid attention to the girl who stepped into saddle of a raw-boned dun stallion.

"Ken," she whispered, a little frightened now, "take care of yourself."

His grin was big brotherly, although he was two years younger than Ann. "Don't worry about me, sis. Just get through to Jon Riley. You'll be doing all of us a big favor."

She whirled the dun away from the door. Iron hoofs rang sharply on the frozen ground. She went through the gate and out of sight, and Ken, about to turn back into the house, caught sight of the man who came to the bunkhouse door.

It was the new man Sam Fisher had hired, Guerney. He had pulled on pants over his underwear. Now he stood in the doorway and watched Ann leave; then he ducked back inside.

Ken remained in the doorway. Guerney dressed in two minutes flat. He and Sam Fisher came out of the bunkhouse together, and the two of them made a run for the corral. They saddled and headed out less than twelve minutes after Ann had gone.

Ken went back into the house. He propped the note Ann had given him on the dining room table. Then he took his coat and his father's rifle, a German Mauser .303, and slipped out of the house.

He saddled a wiry black mare and rode out of Spur's yard for the last time.

Big Sam Fisher glimpsed the rider as he started up the crumbly bank of the coulee and jerked his bronc's head around with cruel strength, sending it scrambling back into the wash. Guerney, coming up behind him, had to turn fast to avoid a collision.

"Told you to head her off here," Big Sam growled. "We keep out of sight until she's up close. I don't want to spook her on that dun stud she's riding—we'd never catch up with her if she got away from us!"

They dismounted, and Sam crawled back to the lip of the coulee and watched the girl riding toward them. If she continued on her present course, she'd pass within yards of where he and Guerney waited.

Guerney edged up beside him. The pounding of the dun's hoofs was close in the still air when Sam Fisher walked out to intercept the girl.

Ann Coleman reined in sharply. Guerney came up and circled behind her, his rifle held ready, a loose grin on his face.

Sam reached up and caught her bridle before she recovered from the shock of seeing them. He was smiling, but his features, lumpy from the bruises he had received, had a mean look.

"Sam! What are you doing here?"

"Waiting for you," Sam answered bluntly.

She tried to jerk the bridle from his grasp. "I'm in a hurry!" she cried. "I've no time for—"

"You'll take the time!" Sam growled. Guerney moved forward, licking his lips.

Fear made her sick. "Sam! Turn my horse loose!"

Spur's ramrod reached up and caught her by the arm. He pulled her roughly from the saddle. Ann fell heavily, and he stood over her, making no attempt to help her. The dun snorted and started to move away, but Sam held onto the bridle, jerking him around.

Ten feet away, Guerney suddenly swore and shifted his rifle to his shoulder. A bullet ploughed the ground close to Sam's feet, and the faint whip crack was blurred by the heavier report of Guerney's rifle. The echoes bounced off the nearby hills.

Sam whirled, his Colt appearing in his fist; his puzzled gaze sought the target of Guerney's shot. A hundred yards off, in the direction from which Ann had come, a riderless horse was heading away from them, stirrups flapping.

The man Guerney had shot lay in a limp bundle on the ground. A rifle lay a few feet from him.

Sam yanked Ann to her feet. Guerney was walking slowly toward the man he had shot. He stood over the body, rifle held ready; then he turned and yelled to Sam. "It's the kid brother! Ken Coleman!"

Ann heard him and tried to break free of Sam. He slid his Colt into his holster and cuffed her roughly, rocking her head until all resistance left her. Her sobs were low, muffled.

"Fool kid probably followed her," he muttered. He lifted his voice. "Let's get started, Guerney."

Guerney headed back at a dogtrot to the coulee where he had left his cayuse. A few minutes later he rode up to Sam, leading the foreman's horse.

Fisher lifted Ann Coleman up to the saddle in front of Guerney. "Take her to the canyon. We'll decide what to do with her later—after Riley comes across the river."

He waited until Guerney and the girl had disappeared through a break in the low, bare hills. Then, leading both his and Ann's horse, he walked to Ken's body.

It was obvious the kid had trailed his sister without her knowledge. Probably curious as to where she was headed. Sam scrubbed his jaw thoughtfully. This had not been planned; yet it could be turned into an advantage.

When he showed up at Spur with Ken's body across Ann's saddle and told his story, every man at the ranch would turn out for blood—for the blood of Jon Riley and the sheepmen waiting across the Longhorn!

Sam had only one small regret, brought alive

by the soreness of his jaw. He was sorry that in the melee at the river, he would not get a chance at the lawman who was the only man to knock Big Sam Fisher off his feet in over a score of vicious brawls.

-XVI-

The snow came in tiny pellets that bounced off their hats, bit into exposed portions of their faces, bounced and ran like tiny white bugs over the frozen ground.

Matt Vickers was following Jed's mule along a pathless route into the hills. The Indian fighter sat like a crumpled sack in his saddle, head hunched between his shoulders. Occasionally a brown streak would eject from his mouth, to splatter against the earth.

Matt was occupied with his own thoughts. Jed had made much of the pattern clear. It was not the first time a trusted foreman had turned crooked and robbed his employer. That Sam Fisher had been able to get away with it for some time was less understandable; it could be explained by the fact that Colt Coleman had been practically an invalid these past two years and had left the running of the ranch to Sam and his daughter Rita.

This much of the pattern fitted. Riley's return to the valley with Milt Gavel and his gunmen must have played into Sam's hands. A war between Riley and Spur could mean only one winner: Sam Fisher and the rustlers who had been stripping Spur.

But some of the pieces of the puzzle were still missing. Matt didn't know what had happened to Riley, or why Riley had sent Reverend Sharon to arrange for a meeting with Ann Coleman. What was Ann Coleman to Jon Riley?

Nor did it explain satisfactorily who had killed the sheriff and shot Dan. And it didn't explain who had taken that shot at Matt through the boarding house window.

Ahead of him, Jed suddenly pulled up, raising his right hand. The chestnut blew softly as Matt reined him in.

Jed dismounted and motioned for the marshal to do the same. They left the animals tied to saplings. Jed brought his buffalo gun with him.

"They been gettin' careless," he whispered. "Usually keep a lookout on them rocks—" he gestured—"an' one of 'em down at the entrance to the canyon. Last two times I been here, they quit postin' a man up here."

Matt nodded grimly. "How many?"

"Counted seven of 'em. Seven with Big Sam. But he don't stay with 'em. Don't expect he'll be here today."

They crawled to the edge of the cliffs and looked down. Almost directly below them was a cabin, a rough log affair with a dirt roof pitched to the rear. A rusty hunk of stovepipe jutted from the offside wall, elbowing up to throw a plume of gray smoke against the cliff face.

Farther down the canyon, a half-dozen horses crowded an open-sided shed. Beyond this the canyon curled away, kidney-shaped, fading into the rocky country. From his vantage point Matt could see no cattle, and he mentioned this to Jed.

"Got rid of the last bunch about four, five days ago," the older man grunted. "They rebrand 'em here an' run 'em through the rough country to some buyer. I didn't track 'em that far. Wanted to keep close to my place in case you showed up."

Matt said, "I'm going down for them. Up here you can pick off any I miss."

Jed squinted at the sky. There was perhaps a half-hour of light left.

"A forty-foot rope will get yuh as far down as that ledge. You kin make it without a rope the rest of the way. There's a winder in the back of the shack, but yuh can't spot it from this angle." He patted his Sharps. "You run 'em out the front door, Marshal—me an' Betsy will show 'em the error of their ways!"

Matt glanced toward the entrance of the canyon, hidden by an abutment of the cliff they were on. "We may have to miss one of the polecats if they have a lookout at the entrance, Jed."

Jed spat. "Might be I could crawl close enough to silence him." He reached back to touch the shaft of his hunting knife.

Matt vetoed the idea. "No time—" He stiffened, his glance picking up the rider who came into view below them. The thin sleet made for poor visibility, but it did not hamper him to the point where he could not make out the girl being held on the saddle in front of the new arrival.

Jed cursed. "That's Ann Coleman, Matt!"

The rider rode to the shack and dismounted, pulling the reluctant girl down. Matt's eyes held a bleak glint. He recognized the stocky man—the second of Pepper's "clients." The pattern suddenly became clear.

He pulled back from the cliff and made his way back to the chestnut. He patted the sleek hide reassuringly as he unfastened his rope.

Crawling back to Jed, he made it secure to a rock jut, then shook the free end over the cliff. He knew what would happen to him if he should be spotted while climbing down, but he had faith in this one-time Indian scout cuddling his Sharps rifle.

Jed said anxiously, "The gal in there ain't gonna make it easy for yuh, Marshal."

Vickers shrugged. "Keep your eyes peeled, Jed." And he went over the side.

The hail stung the back of his neck, bounced off the cliff wall into his face. He lowered himself hand over hand; coming to the end of the rope, he let himself go and dropped seven feet down to the ledge. He landed on flexed legs and straightened immediately, getting his back against the cold rock.

It was less than thirty feet now to the canyon floor. He made it without arousing anyone in the shack.

The rear window had a lower pane broken. A piece of burlap had been stuffed into it to keep out the weather.

The marshal peered through the dirty panes just as someone inside lighted an oil lamp. The glow gave him a clearer view of the shack's occupants.

Four men were sitting on boxes around a bench table, playing cards. The stocky man who had brought Ann into the canyon was standing beside her, near the small iron stove, pouring coffee into a tin cup. Ann was standing with her face in her hands.

Almost directly under Matt a small figure moved. Vickers breathed a sigh of relief as he saw that the Travis boy had not been harmed.

Besides Pepper's stocky "client," Matt recognized only one other man, the small gunman Brazos had called Willy. Brazos was nowhere in sight.

Guerney was talking. ". . . Sitting tight right here. Orders. After Big Sam gets back to Spur with the kid's body an' his story, ole Coleman will throw away his crutch an' head straight for that sheep camp on the Longhorn."

Matt hesitated. He pulled away from the window and moved soft-footed to the front of the cabin. Guerney's winded bronc was standing with drooping head a few feet away; he looked up as Matt appeared. A wary snort blew through his nostrils.

Matt moved swiftly. He caught the animal's trailing reins and jerked roughly. The bronc pulled back, shrilling angrily.

There was a commotion inside the rustlers' shack. The door opened, and Guerney came out, coffee cup in his hand. He didn't see the shadow hugging the side of the door. He started to curse the trembling bronc, and then Matt's palmed Colt dented his hat and he slumped forward.

Matt vanished around the side of the shack. He was at the rear window when the four rustlers came to their feet. One of them called: "Guerney!"

The marshal's Colt was thrust through the lower pane, showering glass into the shack. His voice rode in with the cold wind. "It's four feet to that door—hot lead! Who'll be the first to go?"

Willy, nearest to the lamp on the corner shelf, moved first. His hand swept it off the shelf as he lunged for his holstered Colt; he died before the lamp hit the earthen floor.

The others stampeded for the door!

Lead sent glass over Vickers as he ducked back and cut around the corner of the cabin. From the cliff he heard Jed's rifle boom; he was in front of the building when the Sharps boomed again.

The last man whirled and plunged back toward

the safety of the cabin. He saw Matt appear around the corner and got off one shot before he disappeared inside. Vickers went in after him. Another hasty shot from the desperate rustler chipped wood from the door frame near his face.

Matt stopped short. The rustler had his arm around Ann, holding her in front of him. Along the base of the wall where the lamp had been smashed, the first bluish flicker had strengthened to an orange glow as the fire began to spread quickly up the kerosene-soaked wall.

Matt paused, undecided. The rustler's voice was wild. "Make a wrong move an' she—"

Behind him the Travis boy lunged for the man, his face pinched tight, his eyes closed. He had a sliver of glass in his hand; he jabbed it into the gunman's back.

The man whirled, a cry of pain escaping him. For a moment his head and shoulders were free of Ann. Matt's slug caught him under the left ear.

Dusk came swiftly into the canyon. The burning shack cast a reddish glow into the low, somber sky. The cayuses in the shed, frightened by the fire, tugged at their halter ropes and shrilled wildly.

Jed rode up, leading Matt's chestnut. He looked at Ann Coleman and Buzz Travis standing beside the United States marshal.

"Sentry at the entrance got away," Jed growled. "Looked like it was Brazos."

Matt shrugged. "How far to the sheep camp from here, Jed? Can we make it before morning?"

Jed nodded.

Vickers turned to Ann Coleman. "You were headed there, weren't you?"

Ann nodded. She had recovered somewhat from the shock of what had happened to her and Ken, and her dark eyes gleamed as she looked up at Matt.

The marshal was curious. "You care to tell me why?"

Ann's head lifted proudly. "Because I'm Jon Riley's wife!"

-XVII-

Milt Gavel stirred and came awake. It was still dark. Dawn, Monday's dawn, was still an hour away. He turned and looked at the figure outlined by the window and cursed silently.

Riley had not slept at all!

Milt rolled out of his blankets and pulled on his boots. He had come to like this tall, silent man in the few months he had known him—and he knew what was eating Jon Riley.

He said gruffly: "No use waiting, Jon. She'd have come by now if she was coming at all."

Riley turned. "I guess you're right, Milt." There was no life to his voice.

Milt went over to the stove, rattled the coffeepot and grunted at the sloshing he heard. "Can't sleep myself," he lied. He filled a cup and joined Riley by the window. They had built this temporary shack, and a bigger one for the gunslingers, within sight of the Longhorn. Milt's regular herders were with the sheep, three miles back in a small sheltered valley.

He watched the dark line of the river, and his voice held a leashed excitement. "We move across the Longhorn at daylight, Jon, in spite of Spur!"

Riley said nothing. He was looking into the

185

night, his thoughts long and bitter, reaching back to the more pleasant years he had spent in this valley. He was not a violent man by nature, although he had a grim stubbornness even he had not guessed at.

He had liked it here and had never quite understood what had caused Rita Coleman to do what she had done to him. He had been considerate and pleasant with her, but her aggressiveness, her directness, her almost mannish independence had not interested him. She was Colt Coleman's kind of girl, and in a way Coleman was to blame for what had happened.

Because of her father, Ann had been afraid to marry him. "He thinks you should marry Rita," she had whispered. Her eyes had been dark, tearful. "All my life I've had to face that, Jon—Dad always wants the best for Rita."

"I don't love your sister," he had told her. "It's you I want to marry."

"Dad would never consent to it, Jon. He likes you, but—"

"Then we'll marry without his consent," Riley had replied. And he had prevailed on her. They were married in Reverend Paul Sharon's house, with H. Goldwyn Pepper and Sheriff Earl Wright as witnesses. And both men, as well as the minister, had agreed under oath to keep their secret.

It had been June, and they'd had a brief two

hours together by the far bend of the creek. They had talked of little things and been happy. And then Ann had ridden back to Spur.

Who had told Rita Coleman?

She had come for Riley the next night in her buggy, which was unusual, because Rita seldom drove. Ann wanted to see him, she had told him. And Jon had gone with her along the moonlit road to Spur.

Where a stand of cedar made a dark splash against the trail, Rita had halted the buggy.

"I know about you and Ann being married," she said.

Riley was taken by surprise. "I wanted to tell you," he said. "I wanted your father to know. But Ann was afraid—"

"Poor little defenseless Ann!" Rita's voice was almost hysterical. "She knew how I felt about you, Jon. But she stole you from me—"

"Ann stole me from no one!" Riley broke in roughly. "I like you, Rita. But I have never given you reason to believe that I loved you—"

She had listened to him. It was then that she had done the unexplainable. She had been wearing a soft white silk blouse; before he could stop her she had torn it off. Her voice was wild. "I'll give you reasons, Jon!"

The two men who came riding from the shadows of the cedars had found them like that.

The rest of it was slightly confused to Jon. He remembered being hauled into Spur's yard. Rita's sobbing accusations and Coleman's astonished bellows made little sense. Only Ann's wide, shock-filled eyes haunted him.

They had tied him to a pole, stripped the shirt from his back, and Sam Fisher, who had been one of the two men who had picked him up, had used the whip.

Riley had recovered consciousness sometime during the long ride to the Longhorn. They had dumped him off across the river, left him a saddled horse, and told him flatly that if he ever showed up in the valley again, he'd be shot on sight!

Milt nudged his elbow, and Riley turned slowly to face the reality eighteen months later. The sheepman held out a cup of coffee. "Bitter as sin," Gavel muttered, "but maybe not as bitter as your thoughts, eh?"

Riley took the cup. "Not half as bitter," he admitted.

They heard the riders then, splashing across the Longhorn. Milt set his cup down and scooped up his shotgun. Jon followed him to the door.

The camp was stirring. Men were running out, half dressed, guns drawn. Milt hurried to keep up with Jon.

They came out of the pines and paused to watch the river. There was a pale gleam of pre-dawn light in the night. The riders coming across the river were bunched in a dark mass.

Milt's voice rang out sharply: "Make yourselves known!"

Behind him men were coming through the timber, cursing softly. Rifles glinted as they caught the light.

A voice Milt recognized answered him. "It's Matt Vickers, with Jed Sayer, Buzz Travis—and Ann Coleman!"

Riley stiffened. The riders came on and pulled up a few feet away. A slim figure dismounted quickly and ran to him. He heard her call: "Jon! Jon!" and then he had his wife in his arms!

Dawn paled the sullen sky. The sheep camp was awake, alert. Matt was talking to Milt Gavel.

"There's been enough killing, Milt. When Spur shows up, let *me* handle it."

Gavel looked at his men standing cold and silent around them. They had been hired to fight Spur; they had no real interest in the trouble here, except for what it paid them. But Milt had nursed this moment too long to discard it easily.

"My brother and I were on the Longhorn as long as Coleman," he argued. "And I paid good money for my lease. I have as much right across the river as that old buzzard has!"

"Show me your lease," Matt answered, "and I'll see that the law stands behind you. You'll get across the river, Milt—but it will be legal and without killing."

Milt looked aside toward Jon Riley, standing with Ann by the far end of the camp, under the trees. Riley had found what he had really come after; he would be forgetting the horsewhipping he had received.

Gavel took a long breath. "I could buck Spur," he growled. "But I won't buck the United States government."

Matt held out his hand. He was thinking that it wasn't what a man herded, sheep or cows, that mattered.

A voice broke in on them, sharp and clear. "Here they come! Spur's riding!"

Matt mounted the chestnut and rode for the river. He was in midstream, waiting, when the riders showed up on the far bank.

Sam Fisher was among them, siding Colt Coleman. They pulled up when they saw the tall man with the United States marshal's badge on his coat barring their way.

"That's far enough, Coleman!" Matt's voice rapped out. "I told you to stay on your side of the river!"

"That badge ain't gonna stop me!" Coleman howled. "We've come to get Riley and to wipe out every murdering, stinking sheepherder who—"

He chopped off his raving as Ann appeared

with Riley, walking slowly to the edge of the river behind Matt.

Vickers kneed his horse around so that he faced Spur's ramrod. Sam was looking at Ann as though he were seeing a ghost.

"Tell him, Sam," Matt said. "Tell Coleman who killed the boy. Tell him about the double-cross you've been pulling on Spur, the way you've been stripping his ranges of Spur beef."

The men behind Coleman and Sam were quiet, caught in confusion. Slowly Colt turned his shaggy head to Fisher.

"Tell him," Matt said harshly. "Or do you want Ann to tell him—"

Sam jerked his animal aside and reached for his Colt. Vickers' slug knocked him out of the saddle. He fell heavily, and his cayuse, whirling in fright, stepped on his face.

Vickers holstered his smoking Colt. "Coleman! You can come across the river now—to meet your son-in-law!"

He didn't wait for the reunion. There was no fight left in Spur. Coleman would have a lot of listening to do, and some concessions to make. He'd make some of them willingly, others grudgingly—and some he'd have to be forced into.

But that would be for later. Right now there was one more piece to this puzzle, and he knew he'd find it in Gunsmoke!

-XVIII-

H. Goldwyn Pepper lifted his glass of whiskey and downed it and continued his pompous harangue to a bored bartender. "It is my firm contention, and I will freely repeat it, that—"

The saloon door slammed open, interrupting him. He turned an annoyed glance at the entrant, and at once his manner changed; his eyes grew cold, alert.

Brazos limped in, ignoring the rest of the customers. His tone rasped with grim urgency. "I've got to see you, Pepper."

The lawyer tossed a silver dollar on the bar and jerked a thumb toward the door. "In my office, sir!" But his tone was sharp.

Brazos talked as they walked toward Pepper's office. "All of them wiped out! Willy! Guerney! Slim! Rex!" He cursed violently. "That tall hombre I told you about—the jasper I thought was a drifter who horned in on us at Jed's place—"

"Vickers?"

"Yeah. Guess that's him. He was there. Had someone with him up on the cliffs behind the cabin. Maybe more than one. I didn't hang around to find out. But when I left, the cabin was burning—"

"All right; it's over," Pepper snapped. "Get fresh horses from the livery. Have them in front of my office right away. I'll join you as soon as I clean out what's in my strongbox."

Brazos nodded. "Would have made it into town sooner, but my cayuse stepped into a chuckhole about six miles out." He winced. "My feet are killing me. Sure will feel good to be riding again."

"We'll ride," Pepper agreed. "It's a long haul to the Mexican border."

Brazos hobbled toward the livery stables, and Pepper turned to the flight of stairs by the side of Burke's store. He did not notice the girl who came riding up the street.

He cast off all pretense as he entered his office. He went immediately to his desk, unlocked the bottom drawer and took out a square iron box. It held money from the sale of Spur beef, and it was to have been divided among the rest of the boys when Spur fell.

It was not as much as he had anticipated, but the money would go a long way in Mexico. Brazos expected a share of it. But Brazos would not be with him when he crossed the border.

He opened the box to check it, then locked it again. He found a small leather bag at the bottom of his cabinet and stuffed the box inside. He was crouched over it when he heard the door open. He thought it was Brazos and snarled: "I told you to wait downstairs with the horses—"

"You didn't tell me," the voice said, and Pepper stiffened. He stood in an awkward position, a look of slack surprise on his face. Then he slowly straightened, leaving the bag at his feet.

Rita Coleman left the door open behind her. She was holding a small nickel-plated revolver in her hand, and she looked pale, tired. She had slept very little last night.

"I see I got here in time," she said bitterly.

Pepper tried to bluff it out. "Now, now, Rita, I was just going to Tucson on business."

"With a tin box in an old leather bag?" she shook her head. "The money's in it, isn't it? Money that belongs to Spur." Her voice was tight. "Money I let you have, isn't it? Money you and Big Sam Fisher blackmailed me for. Oh, I was never the fool you thought, Mr. Pepper. I knew what was going on—"

"I'm sure you did," Pepper said. He was thinking of the derringer in his vest pocket and wondering if he could get to it before she shot him.

"I told you I was through. But you didn't believe me. You thought I was just talking—" She moved into the room, and he saw that her face was as tight as a drum and her eyes seemed black.

"Sam killed Jed Sayer, didn't he? He killed

194

Noel Travis, too. I alibied for him, but I knew he did it. I stood by for almost two years while you and Sam did as you pleased."

Pepper licked his lips. "Why the hysterics now, Rita? The self-condemnation? Sure, Sam killed Noel Travis. And I shot Earl Wright. He had called in a United States marshal; he was going to tell him about Sam and the raids on Spur. He was going to tell Vickers about Jon Riley marrying Ann—"

The old hurt was there in her eyes, and he laughed with cruel enjoyment.

"Yes, I knew all that," Rita said. Her voice was thin, ashamed. "But you went too far even for me, Pepper. When you had Ken killed and Ann kidnapped—that was too much!"

Pepper tensed. Fear cut across the laughter in his eyes. "Don't be a little fool," he said quickly. "Let me go. No one will know what happened that night. I promise you."

She shook her head. "It's too late, Pepper." Her voice was low, burning in her throat. "Way too late. Ken's dead, and Dad left for the Longhorn last night. He had a dozen men with him. It's what you and Sam wanted—and it's too late for everyone, Pepper."

He kicked the moneybag toward her, and she fired instinctively. Her shot took a swatch from the shoulder of Pepper's black coat. Then the derringer barked a flat reply, and Rita Coleman jerked and fell against a chair, overturning it.

Pepper picked up the leather bag and headed for the door. He saw Brazos riding toward him leading a saddled horse. No one seemed to have heard the shots.

He tied the bag securely and got into the saddle. He took one last look back as they rode out of town. He knew he would never see it again.

Matt Vickers got into town late in the afternoon. He went directly to Pepper's office and was the first to find Rita Coleman. She wasn't dead. But she was badly hurt.

He picked her up and carried her to the doctor's house. And he stayed with her while Doc Ramsey operated and took out the tiny pellet which lodged under her right breast.

She was conscious for a while, and he told her what had happened at the Longhorn. "Sam's dead," he said. "So are all the men who worked with him."

Her eyes closed. "And Ann?"

"She's with Riley. With her husband."

A sigh escaped her. "You know?"

Matt nodded. "What there is to know." He looked up as Doctor Ramsey frowned and shook his head. He showed the doc a finger, indicating he wanted one more minute with her.

"Rita, it was Pepper who shot you?"

She nodded weakly. Her face was very pale,

ramed by her black hair, and her lips seemed
bloodless and slightly swollen.

"Where did he go?"

"The border. . . ."

He left her in the doctor's house. He still had a
job to do.

A week later Matt Vickers rode back into
Gunsmoke. He had a prisoner riding on a horse
behind him. Brazos had a bandaged head and a
dispirited look.

Matt stayed in town long enough to find Dan
O'Malley recuperating nicely and looking
forward to taking on his new job as sheriff. Then
he rode on to Spur.

Colt Coleman was sitting in a wicker rocker
on his porch. He watched Vickers dismount, take
a leather bag from his saddle and come up the
steps. Brazos was slumped in the saddle.

Some of Spur's crew drifted around. Matt went
up to Coleman, opened the bag and dumped a
tin box in Coleman's lap. "It's yours," he said.
"Money for Spur beef. Goldy Pepper had it with
him when he headed for the border."

Coleman didn't open the box. He let it lie in his
lap, and his grin was wide. "You kill him?"

Matt turned and looked at Brazos. "No. Brazos
got the idea that all was better than half. He killed
Goldy himself, just this side of the Rio."

Ann and Jon Riley came out as he was talking.

Riley looked younger somehow, and grateful. He shook Matt's hand.

"Milt's across the river," he said. He looked at Coleman, who snorted and looked away. "He finally made it across the Longhorn."

Ann was more shy with Matt. "I'm glad you came by," she said. Then, almost in a whisper, "Rita would like to see you."

Matt went into the house. Ann led him to Rita's bedroom, then left. He stood by the bed looking down at Rita, who was propped up on two pillows. She looked better than she had when he had left her.

"I see you're almost recovered." He held his hat in his hands, and the odd thought came to him, as he watched her, that it was Mary he was looking at, when she had been alive and the future had stretched serenely before them.

His voice was grave. "I heard in town you were planning to go East."

She nodded. "After what happened, I can't stay on here. Perhaps, in a few years—" She smiled sadly. "I won't be seeing you again, will I?"

Matt shrugged. How could he answer this girl? "I don't know," he murmured. "Perhaps, some day—"

Her voice was hesitant. "Will you kiss me?"

He looked down at her, knowing what she had been through. She was headstrong, willful, used to getting what she wanted. Yet she had fire and something that appealed to him. He thought of Ann, and the odd reflection came to him: "Each man to his own taste, in women as in liquor."

He bent over and kissed her, finding her lips warm against his, clinging. He straightened finally, more shaken than he had expected to be.

"Goodbye, Rita."

She watched him go—and the sun came through the curtains at her window, brightening up the bleak and lonely room.

Center Point Large Print
600 Brooks Road / PO Box 1
Thorndike, ME 04986-0001 USA

(207) 568-3717

US & Canada:
1 800 929-9108
www.centerpointlargeprint.com